# Frederick the Great and his Merchant

## Vol. II

SALZWASSER
VERLAG

**Klara Mundt**

# Frederick the Great and his Merchant

## Vol. II

Reprint of the original, first published in 1858.

1st Edition 2023 | ISBN: 978-3-37515-170-6

Verlag (Publisher): Salzwasser Verlag GmbH, Zeilweg 44, 60439 Frankfurt, Deutschland
Vertretungsberechtigt (Authorized to represent): E. Roepke, Zeilweg 44, 60439 Frankfurt, Deutschland
Druck (Print): Books on Demand GmbH, In de Tarpen 42, 22848 Norderstedt, Deutschland

# FREDERICK THE GREAT

AND

# HIS MERCHANT.

FROM THE GERMAN,

BY LADY WALLACE.

IN TWO VOLUMES.

VOL. II.

RICHARD BENTLEY, NEW BURLINGTON STREET.

1858.

# FREDERICK THE GREAT

# AND HIS MERCHANT.

---

## EPHRAIM THE JEW.

THERE was much suffering and sorrow for the inhabitants of Berlin in these days of persecution and oppression; but the Jews were, of all classes of the community, the most alarmed, and indeed had most cause for fear. They, who in Berlin, and everywhere else, led a patient, despised, and suffering existence, for whom there were no rights, only duties—no honour, only humiliation—no dignities, only shame and meek submission, were now called on to give up their first and last possession, the only thing which shed a glimmer of light on their poor crushed existence—they were to see their gold and silver wrested from them.

The Russian general demanded from the body of Jews in Berlin a special hearth-tax; and, on their hesitating to comply with his exactions, declaring it to be out of their power to pay so enormous a sum, General von Tottleben caused three of the oldest Jews to be seized and imprisoned, and to be closely watched in the vincent-house in the Brüder Strasse.*

It was hard to despise and blame the poor Jews for their unwillingness to part with their gold, which was at that time equivalent to their very existence, their future happiness, and their family rights. It was gold alone which enabled some individuals at least among them to raise themselves from the dust, and from the humiliation they were compelled to endure—a state to which they had been reduced by "Christian law," obliged to renounce hope, domestic ties, and all the kindly feelings common to humanity. Those only among them who possessed gold were tolerated in Berlin, and could venture to hope, by untiring industry, unceasing activity, and lucky speculations, to amass sufficient wealth

* Biography of a Patriotic Merchant, page 42.

to purchase the right of founding a family, and having children; for this domestic happiness was only vouchsafed to those who were rich.

Frederick the Great had learned with indignation that the number of Jewish families, legally limited to one hundred and fifty-two, had far exceeded that amount, and that at least fifty-one more could be enumerated. He therefore issued a strict order that the Jews should no longer be counted by families, but by individuals; and, when the latter exceeded the legal number, the poorest and humblest Jews were to be mercilessly driven away.*

Gold was therefore to the Jew a security for his home and for his happiness; the poor had not even the shelter of a residence, and at any hour or moment could be banished and forced to leave Berlin; whereas a rich Jew could purchase the right by his money, and his traffic, not only to bring a wife to his household hearth, but to declare himself openly the father of his child.† He dared acknowledge

* Biography of a Patriotic Merchant, pages 42, 43.

† Prussia: Frederick the Great, vol. iii. page 428.

but one child, for one alone was admitted by law. The rich Jew could extend his purchased protection to one child, and only in singular exceptions, when the manufactories and fabrics established by the Jews were peculiarly prosperous, did the King, in the fulness of his favour, sanction a second child inheriting any portion of the father's wealth.*

What availed it then the poor Jews that, impelled by terror and fear for their very existence, they had scraped together sufficient to liquidate the shameful Jewish poll-tax, thus to purchase at least a momentary exemption from persecution? At any moment they might be compelled to wander forth on the earth, homeless and houseless, though the wealthy Ephraim, or the rich David Itzig, in the pride of their successful speculations, were prosperous enough to purchase a brief of exemption by the payment of three thousand dollars.†

* Büsching's Journey from Berlin to Bekahur, Frankfort, and Leipzig, 1780.

† Annals of the Jews in the Prussian States.—Berlin, published by Anger.

It was little consolation even to the rich Ephraim and Itzig that they were wealthy—they were still degraded by the shame of their race; there were no privileges, no offices for them,—their occupations were limited to merchandise or manufactures; and all the other pursuits of life, even agriculture and gardening, were prohibited to their race.* Now they were called on to give up the sap of their life, the nerve of their very being, the heart which diffused blood and warmth through their whole organisation, their chief good—their money, to the Russians.

Ephraim and Itzig were rich and powerful in Berlin; they could build houses, establish

* In an ordinance connected with the Jews, Frederick the Great wrote on the margin with his own hand, "No Jews are to have any privileges; they may establish new manufactories, but the prescribed number of families is not to be exceeded." In another Cabinet order he says, "We learn from your report that the Jews have the audacity to farm cattle; we here declare on this subject that this displeases us, and it is our order that this interference with agricultural pursuits on the part of the Jews should be put a stop to, and never again permitted."

manufactories, and even fix the value of gold, for the mint was in their hands. They had farmed it from the King, and paid an enormous sum for this privilege, which every year increased, and at last, in the year 1760, amounted to seven millions.

Owing to this lease of the mint by the Jews, the value of gold increased so prodigiously that twenty dollars were paid for a Friedrich-d'or, and thirty-five for a mark of fine silver.

Thanks to the efforts of these Jews, there were many millions of light gold coin in circulation, and many millions of bad eight groschen pieces, which are even to this day known by the name of Ephraimites; the withdrawal of which at a later period plunged many thousands of upright and respected merchants into poverty and ruin, while Ephraim, Itzig, and others thus became still more rich and prosperous.

At this moment, however, it was precisely their gold which had brought misfortune on their heads and caused them such a deadly panic and anguish of soul: for General von Tottleben had threatened, if they resisted payment of the tax he had imposed on them, to carry off the Jews of the mint as hostages, first destroying their manufactories. He had, moreover, as we already said, seized some of the oldest of their community, and sworn to send them off to Siberia, there to drag out the remains of their wretched existence, if they persevered in their refusal. The payment was to be made within three days; but this period had elapsed without the poor persecuted Jews being able to collect the enormous sum of solid gold which was exacted from them. In this hour of anguish and need the two principal Jews of the mint, Ephraim and Itzig, thought of the man whom hitherto they had cordially hated, and whose destruction had been the most eager wish of their life. They now remembered that Johann Gotzkowsky was the only man who, in the magnanimity and goodness of his heart, would overlook former insults and offences, and only remember their need and their misfortunes.

They therefore resolved to go to him to implore his support; but, even while doing so, they sighed and felt their rage and hatred against him only increase and surge more mightily than ever within their hearts.

"Who would have thought it," said Ephraim, while going along by Itzig's side, escorted by some of the richest Jewish merchants, to Gotzkowsky's house; "who could believe such a thing? The all-powerful Russian, General Tottleben, is a friend of Gotzkowsky's, and the greatest men among our people must repair humbly to the merchant's house and implore his protection like beggars."

"Yes, we must meekly entreat for his intercession," sighed the rich merchant David; "and yet, what is he compared with you, Ephraim? You are far richer than he is."

Ephraim started, and looked cautiously round—"Hush! you unhappy creature," said he crossly; "I am not only poor, but very poor, therefore I cannot pay. I am badly off, like all Jews. Were we not obliged to contribute more than any one to the war tax? Are not our means fairly exhausted? Is it not enough, and more than enough?"

"Too much, too much!" said Itzig with a sigh, who had hitherto strode along in silence and sadness beside Ephraim. "Do they treat us like men? Have we any rights, any privileges? Only when we are called on to pay do they remember that we have a right, at least, to give away our hard-won property. When the Jew has no money, I tell you, he is no man."

"Oh! as to that," cried Ephraim, "he who has no money is no man, whether he is a Jew or a Christian. If Gotzkowsky had no money, he would be as little considered as we are. Why does the Russian General cultivate his friendship? Because he is rich. Why do princes and counts pay court to him? Because he is rich. Why is his daughter called an angel, and the loveliest girl in Berlin? Because her father is the richest of all the Christian merchants here—the whole world reverences and honours him—and why? because he is rich."

"No man is rich," said Itzig, shaking his head; "he who does not possess everything is not truly rich—there is no solid wealth—for he who has much must give much."

angry tone, "Yes; yes; we must humble ourselves before him, and coax him to listen to us; and yet we are richer than he."

So long as they were passing along the streets these men were full of pride and arrogance, but as soon as they entered Gotzkowsky's house their whole being was transformed into mildness, meekness, and humility; they besought Gotzkowsky to have compassion on them, and to intercede in their favour with General Tottleben. They assured him of their everlasting gratitude, and solemnly vowed that if he succeeded in freeing them from the hearth-tax they would love and esteem him, and be grateful to him for ever and ever.

Gotzkowsky smiled rather scornfully, "Which means," said he, shrugging his shoulders, "that you will never forgive me for having placed you under obligations to me; and if it ever lies in your power you will do all you can to ruin me; but that is no affair of mine at this moment, the hearth-tax is a crying injustice, and therefore I will interfere in your favour; for it shall never be said that Gotzkowsky suffered injustice when he could prevent it. Go home in peace, and if I can I will assist you."

"How proud this man is!" said Itzig, when they had left the house; "he really talks as if he rented virtue and honour for his own sole use—just as we do the mint."

"Well," said Ephraim laughing, "he has only done so to make a good speculation out of them, and he finds virtue as profitable a traffic as we find our money exchange—he will wear it out too just as we are doing our light eight groschen pieces, and deceive the people for his own advantage, exactly as we do."

"Woe to him!" muttered Itzig sourly; "if such a fragment of his virtue ever falls into my hands I will throw it in his face; and I will never forgive him for the way in which we have been this day forced to humble ourselves before him; when his day of need comes I shall not forget it—a Jew without money is no man—we shall see what this arrogant Gotzkowsky is when he has no money; for I tell you we shall find that come to pass yet. He is a vast deal too proud and too lavish not to be one day ruined, and then honour and virtue and all such stuff will not help him. Bosh! we shall hear no more then of the great Gotzkowsky, and his virtues. I shall be glad when the time comes; but it is lucky he has the power to help us now."

## THE RUSSIAN GENERAL AND HIS GERMAN HEART.

THE Jews had scarcely quitted Gotzkowsky's house, when he, still quite absorbed by the intelligence General Bachmann had brought him, repaired to Tottleben's residence, firmly resolved to risk everything to neutralise the cruel order which threatened the manufactories with total destruction. But it was not this purpose alone which brought him to Tottleben. He appeared as the deputy of the whole city. Everyone who required his assistance had applied to him, and he had promised his mediation to all. Loaded with entreaties and complaints from the magistracy, the merchants, and the citizens of Berlin, Gotzkowsky entered the dwelling of the Russian general.

His soul was filled with noble and earnest enthusiasm, and, while he was crossing the hall to the General's audience-chamber, he said to himself, "This is the most important mission of my life, for the welfare of the whole city depends on the result. On each word which I utter hang millions of gold and—of tears. I have fought valiantly of late, but to-day is the most severe struggle of all, and my tongue is the sharp weapon with which I must conquer." Gotzkowsky entered the General's presence with a beaming countenance and sparkling eyes, his whole being imbued with the sacred responsibility of his embassy.

Tottleben did not welcome him in his usual friendly manner, he did not even look up from the despatches which he was reading, and his frowning brows, and the gloomy expression of his features, were, indeed, sufficient to scare away every word of entreaty and supplication.

The General was at this moment wholly Russian, and, thanks to General Fermore's despatches, he had succeeded in hardening and tranquillizing his German heart. He at least hoped and resolved that it should be so, and, therefore, he evidently avoided meeting

Gotzkowsky's clear bright eyes. After he had finished reading the papers, he stood up, and, without noticing his visitor, began to pace up and down the room. Then, as if by chance, he appeared to perceive his visitor, and stopped short.

"What! you here again?" asked he, in an irritable, sulky voice. "I suppose you want to remonstrate about some other paltry stuff. I cannot bear such constant begging and praying. Miserable creatures! always crawling at our feet."

"I agree with your Excellency," said Gotzkowsky, smiling, "the Russians are poor creatures, and are despised by all Europe; they prostrate themselves before their superiors like dogs, and are rude and insolent to the poor and lowly. I am quite of your opinion."

"I was not speaking of the Russians," cried the general, turning his gloomy face towards Gotzkowsky. "I was speaking of you. The whole day you do nothing but ask and demand." Gotzkowsky met his angry looks with entire composure. "Pardon me, your Excellency, *you* demand, and, precisely because you do, I am equally obliged to ask in my turn," said he; "and, in point of fact, when I do so it is for your sake also."

Tottleben looked at him in considerable surprise, but said nothing. Gotzkowsky continued: "I do not entreat for any favour, simply for justice; and, when you grant this, it is a gain for yourself, your Excellency; the world will esteem you not only for being brave, but also for being just, and history will hereafter duly honour him as truly great who, in the hour of victory, showed himself to be just and humane. The Vandals, too, conquered by the sword, and, if brute strength alone were to be victorious, wild bulls let loose would be the greatest heroes."

Tottleben cast a furious look at him, and said, in a threatening voice, "A precious fool he must be who dares to bait such a bull!"

Gotzkowsky bowed and smiled. "It is true," said he, "you must never show him a scarlet cloak; you must tame him by a fearless, resolute eye. The bull is powerless against the spell which fetters him from the eye of man."

Perhaps it was the very boldness of this answer which pleased the General, so accustomed to Russian slavishness.

His features suddenly assumed a softer expression, and, turning quickly to Gotzkowsky, he said, in a milder tone, "You are a strange being, and it is no use contending with you. You must always have your own way. Tell me at once what you want from me?"

"Justice!" cried Gotzkowsky. "Your Excellency gave me your word that your soldiers should neither rob nor plunder, and yet they do both."

"That is not true," cried the General, in a voice of thunder.

"It is true!" said Gotzkowsky, calmly.

"Who dares to contradict me?" cried Tottleben, as trembling with rage he went up close to Gotzkowsky.

"I dare!" said Gotzkowsky firmly; "if, indeed, you consider it daring on my part to undeceive your error. I have myself seen your soldiers strike down poor helpless women with the butt ends of their muskets, and rush into their houses, ravaging and plundering everywhere. Your orders are badly fulfilled, and your soldiery now almost equal the Austrians in ruthlessness and cruelty."

A smile crossed Tottleben's face. Gotzkowsky had known well how to moderate the General's wrath.

"Only *almost!*" said he. "Woe to my soldiers if they ever equal the Austrians in barbarity."

He paced the room restlessly for a few minutes, and then summoned his aide-de-camp.

"Despatch patrols into the streets," commanded he, when the aide-de-camp entered. "Give the strongest orders to the men to preserve the strictest discipline. If any one dares to plunder, he acts contrary to martial law, and he shall be instantly tried and punished by that law,—the gallows for thieves and marauders! Say this to my regiments, and well do they know that General Tottleben will keep his word."

"Are you satisfied now?" asked he, turning to Gotzkowsky when his aide-de-camp had left the room.

"I thank your Excellency sincerely," said Gotzkowsky, hesitating.

"Now, Heaven be praised, that you are contented at last, and have nothing more to ask!" exclaimed Tottleben gaily.

"Indeed, your Excellency, I have a great deal more to ask," said Gotzkowsky; "but, with your permission, I will first address one question to you. You have just issued an order to your army. To what rank does this order extend? Is it to be put in force with regard to privates alone, or must the highest in rank, as well as the most lowly, submit to it?"

"I should like to see any one dare to disobey it!" exclaimed Tottleben angrily. "The order extends to every man in the army."

"Even to officers of the highest rank?"

"Certainly; Generals themselves are not exempt."

Gotzkowsky went a step nearer the General, and said in a distinct voice, "Then, your Excellency, I accuse before you an officer who dares to act contrary to the terms of your order. You have strictly prohibited robbery and plunder on pain of instant punishment, and yet this officer commits both. You have commanded the army to preserve the most exact discipline, and not to maltreat and injure the defenceless; and yet a General does both."

Tottleben had become pale from rage. "The name!" cried he furiously; "the name instantly!"

"General von Tottleben," said Gotzkowsky deliberately.

Tottleben stepped back in horror, and stared at him.

Gotzkowsky did not cast down his eyes, but encountered the General's enraged looks with perfect calmness.

"Are you out of your senses?" asked the general, after a long pause. "Do you find life such a burden, and that you are resolved to lose it?"

"My falling head would only furnish another proof of the truth of what I maintain," said Gotzkowsky solemnly, "that General Tottleben issues an order to his army, but does not himself respect it; that he forbids his soldiers to plunder or to rob on pain of death, and yet he does not hesitate to do both himself."

The very excess of this audacity had precisely the effect on the General's mind which Gotzkowsky expected, and on which he had speculated—knowing Tottleben's lion nature—who, instead of instantly causing his bold aggressor to be seized, rather felt satisfaction at this insolence. It showed him that Gotzkowsky thought his nature too noble to revenge such offensive words.

"Hearken, my friend!" said he. "You are so audacious that you make me laugh! For the sake of singularity I will hear you further, and endeavour to retain my equanimity. Speak on; but I tell you to take care that you prove your words. Accuse me if you will, but woe to you if I can justify myself."

"A German proverb says, 'Small thieves are

hung, great ones escape,'" said Gotzkowsky, shrugging his shoulders. "You wish to prove the truth of this proverb, your Excellency. The soldiers who enter a house by force are punished, but the General remains unpunished who devastates a whole city, and who in the pride of victory renders himself immortal—like Erostratus—by fire."

"Do not try my patience too far," interrupted Tottleben, raising his arm with a threatening gesture towards the bold speaker; "Erostratus desecrated a temple!"

"You have done no less," cried Gotzkowsky, boldly. "You have with impious hand thrown a firebrand into the holy temple of industry: Erostratus destroyed only the temple of a fabulous god; but you wish to raze to the ground our manufactories. Do you know what that means? It means, depriving the poor man of the daily bread which he earns in the sweat of his brow for his wife and child, rendering unavailable his only possession, bodily strength, robbing him of his only privilege, the right to labour; you have doomed to destruction the gold and silver mints; you intend to raze to the ground the arsenals; you are resolved to demolish the copper manufactory in Neustadt Eberswalde; and whence all this barbarism? Why do you resolve to leave behind you such monuments of your Vandalism? Because your Empress is at variance with our King?"

"Because an enemy has a right to avenge himself on another enemy," interrupted Tottleben, angrily.

"Be it so!" cried Gotzkowsky, eagerly. "Revenge yourself on your enemies if you consider the ruthless destruction of property a noble revenge. Destroy the royal palaces, rob the King if you will of his most noble enjoyment, of his pictures; imitate the Saxons in their ferocity, who yesterday ravaged Charlottenburg; send your soldiers to my house; splendid works of art hang on my walls which I purchased by command of our King in Italy, and which his majesty is charmed with the idea of one day transferring to Sans Souci. Revenge yourself, carry off these pictures, set fire to noble works of art, but not to the property of the poor."

He spoke with noble enthusiasm, with glowing eloquence, and, in spite of himself, Totleben's genuine feelings revived within him, urging him to mildness and mercy; but the despatches of General Fermore lay before him, and forced him to sternness and cruelty.

"You think you are talking the perfection of wisdom, whereas, in my opinion, you are talking the extremity of folly," said he, with assumed indignation. "Who has any thoughts of injuring the property of the poor? The King's possessions shall be destroyed, but nothing more."

"The gold and silver mints and the arsenal are not the property of the King," cried Gotzkowsky, eagerly; "not a single dollar from that source flows into the King's treasury."

The General's face brightened, and he repeated in almost a joyful tone; "Not into the royal treasury? where then?"

"That money, your excellency," said Golzkowsky, solemnly, "has a noble and touching destination; you are a father yourself, and when you go into battle you pray for your children, and commend them to the protection of God, that they may not be left orphans."

Tottleben muttered some inaudible words and made a deprecatory gesture—his lips trembled, and, incapable of concealing his emotion, he turned aside.

Gotzkowsky cried joyously, "Do not attempt to hide your real feelings, nor vainly attempt to look sternly at me. Spare the poor children. The produce of the gold and silver mints and of the arsenal is devoted to the support of the new large orphan establishment in Potsdam. You cannot be so barbarous as to deprive the poor children, whose fathers war has already snatched away, of their last refuge, their last support."

The General approached him, and seized his hand. "God is my witness," said he, in a faltering voice, "that such is not my intention; but are you certain of the fact? is this literally true?"

"Yes! General! it is the simple truth."

"Will you swear it?"

"With the most sacred oaths."

The General was silent and thoughtful, for a few moments, and then, placing his hand on Gotzkowsky's shoulder, he said, kindly, "My good friend, I am not unfrequently reproached in my adopted country with being too tender-hearted and compassionate; I will once more, however, follow the impulses of pity, and act contrary to the orders I have received. You must assist me in my object. Place on paper what you have just told me. Say, that these manufactories are not royal property, but belong to the Institution for Orphans, confirmed by an affidavit, and add your seal and signature to the document. Will you do this?"

"Joyfully!" cried Gotzkowsky, his face beaming with pleasure; "I shall never have given my signature so gladly as to this attestation, which will call forth many blessings on both our heads, your Excellency, from many young hearts."

He went to the General's writing table, and,

according to his wish, seated himself and began to write.

Tottleben's face was mild and thoughtful, and no trace of his former wrath was visible.

Once he murmured, in a low voice, "The rights of orphans should be sacred. Elizabeth has a gentle heart, and when she hears my reasons for not obeying she will be satisfied. Yes, I feel I am doing right in acting thus."

"I have finished, your Excellency," said Gotzkowsky, rising and reaching him the prescribed paper.

Tottleben read it over carefully, and placed it beside the despatches of the Empress. He then called his aide-de-camp, and commanded him instantly to place a strong guard on the mint and arsenal to protect them from danger.*

Gotzkowsky clapsed his hands and looked up to Heaven with grateful joy; in the deep emotion of his heart he did not observe that

* Biography of a Patriotic Merchant, page 44. Gotzkowsky alone, in reality, saved the doomed buildings by his intercession.

the General was again standing close to him, and looking at him with kind sympathy.

"Are you satisfied now?" asked Tottleben.

Gotzkowsky shook his head, smiled, and said, "Satisfied, your Excellency! no one is satisfied till he lies in his coffin."

The General's brow became overclouded.

"So!" said he, "pray do not be on any ceremony on that point."

"In asking further favours, your Excellency?" said Gotzkowsky, smiling.

"No, in lying down as soon as possible in your coffin," said he roughly.

"I have no time for that at present," said Gotzkowsky, gravely; "we have both still much to do, your Excellency; you have many laurels yet to add to your former ones. As for me, my duty is to endeavour still to remove many thorns and thistles from the path of my fellow-countrymen."

"So, there are still some thorns?" asked Tottleben, sinking into a chair, and contemplating Gotzkowsky with visible dissatisfaction.

"A great many, General," answered Gotzkowsky, with a sigh, "our whole frame is bleeding from them."

"Then call on the Evil One to heal you," said the General, impatiently.

"You alone can heal us," answered Gotzkowsky, gravely, "for you are about to inflict on us the most deadly wound of all; not satisfied with having conquered and humiliated us, you persevere in crushing us in the dust; you have given orders to disarm the militia of Berlin. You are a brave soldier, and prize your honour beyond all else. I ask you if you are mad thus to furnish proofs to posterity of your pusillanimity. You look angrily at me; you are indignant that I dare even put such a question to you; and yet you wish to impose this disgrace on the citizens of Berlin. We have fought with our weapons for our good cause and for our freedom—it has been the will of Providence, however, that we should be defeated, and that you should be our conqueror; but it would honour you more to be the victor of men than of cowards and slaves. If you demand that we, the conquered, should give up our arms and our honour, we must be miserable cravens, and it is no great deed to have vanquished us. Leave us, therefore, our arms, your Excellency; let us have the consolation of knowing that on our tombstones may be inscribed, 'Liberty perished, but with arms in her hand.'"

Gotzkowsky, overpowered by the painful feelings which tortured his heart, paused and leant against the wall breathlessly, gazing with imploring looks at the General.

Tottleben, however, avoided meeting his glance; he frowned heavily, and kept his eyes steadily fixed on the ground.

Gotzkowsky saw the irresolution of the General, and felt that he must risk the utmost to conquer Tottleben's resistance.

"Oh! leave us our arms, your Excellency," repeated he; "you are by birth a German, oh! spare your German brethren."

Tottleben sprung from his chair as if a poisonous adder had stung him. His features were gloomy and stern; his eyes shot forth angry glances, and, raising his clenched right hand threateningly, he said. "You remind me, in an evil hour, that I once was German. My native country drove me to seek in foreign lands the justice and the appreciation which my Fatherland denied me. Had I been a foreigner, Germany would long since have proclaimed my fame; but, because I was one of her own sons, my Fatherland forsook me, and drove me forth—and this was German love!" and the General broke forth into a loud angry laugh.

"It is, alas! too true," said Gotzkowsky sorrowfully, "that Germany loves to send forth her mighty sons on foreign pilgrimages to win fame. For her great men she has only a cradle and a grave. But prove to your unloving mother, Germania, that you are more noble than herself; show her that she has been unjust! Be magnanimous! Leave us our arms."

"I cannot; by Heavens, I cannot!" said Tottleben with emotion. "There are those above me whom I am bound to obey—the Empress, the General-in-Chief Count von Fermore. I have very strict and severe orders, and I have already granted too much. This despatch contains the express command—arms to be delivered up."

"Arms," said Gotzkowsky hastily; "but it is not written *all* arms. Be satisfied with some. We have three hundred useless muskets—take them, your Excellency; then the letter of your order will be fulfilled, and our honour saved."

The General did not immediately answer, but looked occasionally at Gotzkowsky with a searching glance, whose proud and noble countenance evidently pleased him.

He suddenly said in a scarcely audible voice—

"You think that the Germans would be grateful to me if I acted thus?"

"All Germany would say, He was great in battle, but greater still in magnanimity towards the conquered!" cried Gotzkowsky eagerly.

The General for a time stood motionless. When he again looked up his face had assumed a milder expression.

"Well," said he, "I will do it. I will once more remember that I am a German by birth. Where are the three hundred muskets?"

"In the arsenal, your Excellency."

The General did not reply, but smiled, and went to his writing-table. He hastily wrote a few lines, and again called for his aide-de-camp loudly. When he entered the General gave him the written paper.

"The disarming is to be instantly proceeded with," said he. "There are not more than three hundred muskets available. The citizens are to bring them to the castle square. There they are to be destroyed, and thrown into the Spree."*

When the aide-de-camp had left the room

* Gotzkowsky relates this in his usual natural simple manner as follows:—

"The count excused this order with regard to the delivering up of all arms by Graf von Fermore's severe instructions, but consented, at my earnest entreaty, to allow some hundreds of rusty muskets to be collected in the market-place, to be thrown into the Spree by the Cossacks, so that at least the appearance of having executed the order might be preserved. I immediately went to the magistrate to tell him what I had contrived, and the matter was carried out according to Tottleben's orders."

Gotzkowsky respectfully seized the General's hand, and said in a glad voice—

"Oh! General, believe me, I never in the course of my life felt such sincere and deep gratitude to mortal man as I do to you at this moment. What balm to my heart to be able now to say, Berlin is conquered, but not dishonoured!"

Tottleben nodded kindly, saying—

"After so many proofs of kindness on my part, I suppose I may feel secure that the city will hasten to pay the war contribution I imposed?"

Observing the gloomy cloud which at these words obscured Gotzkowsky's brow, he continued more vehemently—

"You seem very dilatory in its payment beware of abusing my patience."

"You must tell me, your Excellency, when it is fairly exhausted," answered Gotzkowsky. "It is cruel to strain the powers of the exhausted—you agree with me?"

The General bowed his assent in silence.

"You are of my opinion, your Excellency,"

cried Gotzkowsky. "Then you must be just, and not demand from this exhausted, persecuted city more than she can afford to give."

He explained to the General, with glowing words and persuasive eloquence, the impossibility that the city should pay the exacted contribution of four millions.

General Tottleben allowed himself once more to be over persuaded.

His patriotic feelings had been again aroused by the eloquence of this ardent German patriot, and he was disposed to compassion and mildness. He agreed to reduce the war contribution to two millions of dollars, provided that Gotzkowsky would pledge himself that the bills granted by the Merchants' Guild should be punctually met, and that two hundred thousand dollars, as a douceur, should be instantly paid to the Austrians in solid gold.

Gotzkowsky joyfully accepted these conditions, and declared himself ready to become answerable for the payment of these large sums.*

* Biography of a Patriotic Merchant.

Both were for a few minutes silent, equally exhausted by their long and eager struggle of words, in which however Gotzkowsky had been each time victorious. The General was standing at the window looking out into the street. Perhaps he expected that Gotzkowsky would come up to him to express his eloquent and delighted gratitude while taking leave of him. But Gotzkowsky did neither. He stood with folded arms, deep gravity depicted on his noble face, his eye beaming with lofty resolution. "I will finish what I have begun," said he to himself; "I will fulfil my pledge, and not stir from this spot till I have interceded for all those to whom I have promised my mediation. The General may anathematize my importunity, provided only my unfortunate fellow citizens are satisfied with my zeal."

As he remained so long silent, the General turned to him laughing, and said, "Well, have you become dumb? Is your fit of eloquence at an end? Really, when I think of all that you have wrested from me to-day I cannot help laughing," bursting into a good-humoured laugh.

"Laugh away, your Excellency," said Gotzkowsky, "you like hilarity! You have proposed a very amusing joke to the Jews, in imagining they are to pay a hearth-tax.

"Imagining!" interrupted Tottleben, hastily. "My good friend, rest contented with my having remitted two millions to the citizens: don't attempt to advocate the cause of the Jews."

"But the Jews form part of the citizens."

"Are you mad, my good fellow?" cried the general, angrily; "a Jew form part of your community?"

"So far as payment of money is concerned, certainly he does so. The Jews must contribute their fair share to the war contribution, so how can you, with any appearance of justice, demand that they should pay other and different taxes, when they have given up, like ourselves, all they possess?"

"Sir," cried Tottleben, with assumed indignation, "enough, and more than enough!"

"No! your Excellency—too much," answered Gotzkowsky, smiling; "the Jews cannot pay this exaction."

"Then I will remit this hearth-tax!" cried the general, stamping impatiently on the floor: "I will release them from it to please you; simply to get rid of your importunity."*

"Now, however," interrupted Gotzkowsky, in a coaxing tone, "I have only one more favour to ask."

The General stepped back in consternation, and looked at Gotzkowsky with a degree of comic surprise.

"Not satisfied yet?" asked he: "Do you know I begin to fear you must be insane, and shall be truly thankful to get quit of you at last."

"Then you feel towards me," said Gotzkowsky, laughing, "exactly as the city of Berlin does towards you."

The General laughed. "Your audacity is truly astonishing," said he: "well, tell me quickly what is your last request?"

"You are preparing in the Neumarkt a singular and unprecedented spectacle," said Gotzkowsky, gravely: "a spectacle, General,

* Prussia: Frederick the Great, vol. ii. p. 255.

yet unknown to us in Germany—you brought it from Russia with you. You have sentenced two men to run the gauntlet—not two soldiers who have committed a crime, but two authors, who have trespassed against you by their writings, but who have only exercised the fair and honest right of man—*the right to say what they think.* You doom these newspaper editors to be beaten with rods because they took the field against you with their pens. May this not be considered exercising a barbarous revenge for a very trivial offence?"

"A trivial offence!" cried the General, whose face had again resumed a fierce and angry expression, "enough, enough! don't say another word, unless you wish me to retract all I have this day granted you. You think theirs a trivial offence: Sir, the editor of the Spenner newspaper called me an adventurer and a renegade; he shall at least find that this adventurer has the power to punish him."

"Which will only prove to him that he wounded you to the quick," said Gotzkowsky, calmly.

"And that other scribbler of the Voss newspaper," continued the General, wholly absorbed in his wrath, "did he not dare even to attack our gracious Empress? Sir, I am astonished that you condescend to plead the cause of a man who, in a scurrilous pamphlet, assails not only the honour of the Russian Empress, but has equally calumniated your own King."

"Our King is great enough to bear the attacks of meaner souls," said Gotzkowsky. "He who is truly great does not shrink from freedom of speech, nor even from calumny. Have you never, your Excellency, heard the story of our King riding along a street, at the corner of which a crowd of people were assembled, stretching their necks to read a printed paper pasted up high on the wall containing an attack on the King himself? The King checked his horse and read it. The people stood in silence and confusion around, for the paper contained a scurrilous attack on the Sovereign in verse. What do you think, your Excellency, the King did after he had read this treasonable placard?"

"He cut the mob to pieces as they deserved, and hung the author on the highest gallows he could find," cried the General.

"Not at all, your Excellency. He said, 'The people cannot read this poem if it is placed so high up. It ought to be put lower down on the wall.' He then greeted the crowd, and rode away quietly, smiling."

"The great Fritz did that?" said Tottleben, involuntarily having recourse to the epithet which the Prussian people had adjudged their King.

"He acted thus because he was the great Fritz!" said Gotzkowsky.

"Singular! almost incredible!" muttered the General.

A long pause ensued. At last Gotzkowsky said, gently, "Are you disposed to imitate the magnanimity of the great Fritz?"

Tottleben seemed to awake from a reverie. He approached Gotzkowsky, and placed his hand on his shoulder. The expression of his countenance was mild and gentle, and a mournful smile played round his lips. "Listen," said he. "I believe it would be a good thing for me if we were more together. Come with me and settle in Russia. The Empress has often heard of you, and I know she would rejoice were you to come to Saint Petersburg. Do so, I entreat. The favour of the Empress will insure you prosperity. You may attain the highest distinctions; and stars and orders will be showered on you, and a Count's title."

Gotzkowsky could scarcely repress a smile of scorn. "Orders and titles for me?" asked he. "What should I do with them? General, I am more powerful than all your nobles; for the greatness of nobility is derived from the past,—from ancestors now mouldering in the dust; but the greatness of the merchant lies in the future, and that future belongs to industry. I am myself the ancestor of a race to come. I have founded here in Berlin the first extensive manufactories, and those who succeed me will consider me their great original progenitor. I ask for no other nobility, your Excellency."

"Do you really mean that you would actually

refuse the title of count?" said Tottleben, in surprise.

Gotzkowsky shrugged his shoulders. "If I had any wish to become a count," said he, "I could long since have purchased the title from our own realm, for such things are saleable, and such a distinction costs not more than 30,000 gulden; and as for the stars and orders, I have a manufactory myself in Berlin where the ribbons for these toys are made."

The General looked at him long in silence, and with undisguised admiration. "You are a strange man," said he, "and, I sincerely wish I could imitate you. If I had thought like you my life would have been a less stormy one, and less harassed by anxiety and care. I would have" ——

The hasty entrance of an aide-de-camp interrupted the General. He brought despatches which had just arrived, and reported, that the courier had ridden so hard, that his horse had dropped down dead under him at the moment he reached his destination.

Tottleben tore open the papers, and glanced

through them hurriedly. When he again raised his eyes his face had assumed a very different aspect. There was none of the previous mildness and emotion visible there. The feelings of an originally kind heart were stifled by the iron will incumbent on a Russian general. He appeared quite to have forgotten Gotzkowsky's presence, and turning hastily to the aide-de-camp, said, in a brusque military tone, "These despatches are of a very important and surprising nature. They announce that the Prussian army is approaching rapidly by forced marches, with their King at their head. We cannot offer him battle here, and must therefore at once prepare for a speedy retreat from Berlin. Call together all the Generals and their different staffs. Sound the alarm. In the space of three hours the whole army must have quitted the city. Announce our intention to the magistracy in the Neumarkt that we may take leave of them ; for we intend to quit Berlin not as fugitives, but as conquerors, who voluntarily pursue their onward path."

"And the two unhappy editors, who are

about to run the gauntlet?" asked Gotzkowsky, when the aide-de-camp had left them.

The General smiled, and kindly pressed Golzkowsky's hand. "We will hang them a little lower down," said he, significantly. "Come along, you must accompany us to the market place."*

* Graf von Tottleben suffered severely for his forbearance towards Berlin. He was arrested some months afterwards, and sent to St. Petersburg as a prisoner. He was accused, as a Russian general, of having acted in the interests of Germany. The chief accusation was his mildness towards Berlin.

## THE EXECUTION.

The morning was cold and rainy, the wind rushed howling through the deserted streets, making the windows clatter, and doors shut with a crash.

Certainly the weather was little calculated to tempt people into the streets, and yet streams of persons were seen pouring along towards the Neumarkt, unheeding wind and rain, and crowding together in thick masses.

The Berlin people are naturally curious, and never fail to rush to any unusual spectacle. On this day, however, they were destined to see a strange sight.

The editors of both Berlin journals were to run the gauntlet with sticks, and Tottleben had, moreover, ordered the magistracy and the Jews of Berlin to repair to the same spot, to receive his last commands before he left Berlin with his army.

There was, therefore, great excitement and curiosity to witness this double spectacle, and the show loving crowd—the people—rushed by hundreds to the Neumarkt, forgiving the invading General all the horrors and terrors of the previous days, in consideration of the pleasing pastime he was about to grant them.

Two gentlemen of distinction, two learned philosophers, were to be flogged! That was, indeed, a precious and welcome sight for the poor, ragged, hungry, starving wretches to whom it is ever a pleasure to see those plunged into sorrow, or suffering, whom fate had originally placed in a more enviable position than their own. How often had these worthy shoemakers and tailors criticised those newspaper gentlemen over their cans of beer, pronouncing them to be most rash and foolish to write with such violence against the Russians, without adverting to the fact that they might one day arrive in Berlin, and wreak their revenge for all these insults on the poor innocent inhabitants. They thought it served these gentlemen editors quite right to be punished for their insolence.

Besides, the curious mob wished to see the Russian general and his suite and their worthy Berlin magistracy, and their respected Mayor with his heavy gold chain, who, in solemn procession, was to offer to the invading general a present of ten thousand ducats in the name of the city.

The good people of Berlin were therefore quite happy and pleased when they heard the muffled rolling of drums and the Russian word of command given. A regiment of Russian soldiers was just turning the corner of the Bischofs Strasse, and marching in measured step and in profound silence. They placed themselves in two long lines, in the middle of which a narrow passage was left free, only large enough to admit of a man passing along it. Then came two provost marshals, walking slowly down the line, and each soldier drew out a long thin rod from a bundle which the provost marshals carried under their arms.

The Russian soldiers were now armed, and only awaited their victims to commence the punishment. These were dragged forth from the guardhouse. The grey haired Herr Krause comes forward slowly and groaning pitifully; then follows Herr Kretschmer, the once bold and undismayed knight of the pen, now a poor, trembling, dismayed creature. They are placed in the centre of the Markt Platz, and, half maddened by terror, their imploring glances wander over the gaping, silent crowd, who, with eager faces and malicious joy, stare at them, and would be furious if they were deprived of the agreeable excitement of seeing two of their fellow-citizens well cudgelled by the foreign soldiers.

"I cannot believe it even now," said Herr Krause, faintly; "it is impossible that they should be in earnest; so cruel a sentence can never be executed. What will the world —what will mankind in general—think, if two editors are to be nearly beaten to death on account of certain articles in their papers! Can the city of Berlin permit this? Will no man take compassion on us in our extremity?"

"No one," said Kretschmer, sorrowfully. "Look at the crowd staring at us with pitiless curiosity. They would feel more pity for a murderer who was being led to the gallows than for us at this moment. The whole city has read and enjoyed our articles, and now, when we are about to suffer in consequence of them, there is not one single soul who would care to intercede for us."

At this moment a fresh solemn procession arrived by the Bischof Strasse in the Markt Platz. This consisted of the magistracy of Berlin. At their head walked the mayor, Von Kircheisen, who had regained the use of his speech and his faculties, and was inwardly repeating the well-framed address with which he was to convey to the Russian general the thanks of the city, and the 10,000 ducats as a mark of their gratitude, which a page bore on a silk cushion beside him. Behind the magistrates crawled along, in trembling fear and with sorrowful hearts, the elders of the Jewish community and the Jews of the Mint, to receive their final and definitive doom, for good or evil, from General Tottleben.*

The crowd paid little attention either to the magistrates or to the groaning, lamenting Jews who followed them. They kept their eyes intently fixed on the two unhappy editors, whose coats and waistcoats had just been removed by the provost marshals, to prepare them for their bloody punishment. They listened, even with a degree of cruel enjoyment, to the groans of the trembling old man Krause, imploring mercy from the Russian officer charged with the execution of the sentence.

The Russian officer was touched by the heart-rending prayers of the grey-haired editor of the Spenner paper. The bent figure and white locks of the old man inspired him with compassion; or perhaps he only followed Tottleben's private instructions. He made a sign to the provost marshals to lead the editor of the Voss paper first into the narrow ranks of the ap-

* Biography of a Patriotic Merchant, page 41.

pointed regiment, and to spare Herr Krause at least till Kretschmer was sufficiently punished. The provost marshals therefore seized Kretschmer, and, dragging him to the regiment, pushed him between the rows of soldiers, who were loudly laughing and flourishing their rods.

The first, second, and third strokes had already fallen on the back of the unhappy Kretschmer, when a loud "Halt!" resounded, and General Tottleben appeared, with Gotzkowsky by his side, followed by his brilliant staff.

Herr Kretschmer extricated himself, with a loud cry, from the clutches of the provost marshals, and rushed up to the General. Herr Krause, too, started out of his gloomy and despairing state of misery, and both editors sunk at the feet of the Russian General, imploring mercy in the most abject manner.

Tottleben looked with malicious pleasure at the bleeding wounds on Kretschmer's back, and said, proudly, "Pray, who are you, gentlemen?"

"I am the Voss paper, which accused you of

so many dreadful things," whimpered Kretschmer. "Alas! we have been most unfairly used, and depicted as much worse than we are in reality. Believe me, your Excellency, I never hated Russia in my heart."

"You are both accused of having circulated the vilest calumnies," said Tottleben, sternly.

"If we have done so, it has been unconsciously," said Krause; "and we are quite ready to recal all we have said. We were in error, and we are only too glad to acknowledge it. We did not then know either you or your army, and we spoke of both as a blind man does of colours. Now our eyes are opened! You are the most noble of the noble, and finer soldiers than the Russians never were seen, nor a more chaste Empress than Elizabeth. The Spenner newspaper is ready to retract every word! Only prevent my being beaten, honoured General, and I will sing your praises now and for ever more, and proclaim to the whole world that Prussia has no better nor truer friend than Russia and her people, and that they are destined by Providence to become brethren. Only for Heaven's sake do not let me run the gauntlet any further!" implored Kretschmer, rubbing his back, "Have pity on me, and my paper shall become as harmless as a new born babe."

The General turned from him with a smile of contempt. "Enough, gentlemen," said he, roughly; and laying his hand on Gotzkowsky's shoulder, he continued, "I do not pardon you on account of your flow of words, but owing to the intercession of this high-minded and honourable man. You are free, gentlemen!"

When the two editors wished to pour out their expressions of gratitude to Tottleben, he said "You have to thank Gotzkowsky alone for your freedom." *

They threw themselves into Gotzkowsky's

* The poor old editor of the Spenner paper was long on a sick bed from the anguish and misery he had suffered, but eventually recovered, and survived these events seven years.—Events of the Mark of Brandenburg, published by Kosmann and Heinsius, vol. i. p. 79.

arms, and swore everlasting gratitude to him with the most solemn oaths—they called him their saviour and their protector from shame and disgrace.

Gotzkowsky smiled at their glowing assurances of friendship, and extricated himself gently from their eager embraces.

"I did not act thus for the sake of your gratitude," said he, "you are therefore by no means bound to thank me."

"Gotzkowsky! have you quite forgotten us?" asked a melancholy voice close to him. It was Itzig, one of the rich Jews of the Mint, to whom Gotzkowsky had promised his support.

"Ask the General himself," answered Gotzkowsky, smiling.

"Gotzkowsky has interceded for you, and his advocacy has freed you from the hearth-tax," said Tottleben.

"He has saved us! The great Gotzkowsky has taken compassion on our misery," cried the Jews, joyfully pressing towards him, seizing his hand, and embracing him with tears of thankfulness, and vowing never ending devotion.

"You have saved my life," said Itzig, "for I had resolved sooner to die than to pay away any more money—what could I have done with my life if I had no more gold? If a Jew has no money he is no man. You have saved more than my life, you have saved my gold! If the day should ever arrive, Gotzkowsky, when you require money yourself, come to me, and I will lend it to you at a moderate percentage."

"I will lend it to you without any interest at all," cried Ephraim, pressing Gotzkowsky's hand warmly.

Gotzkowsky said, with a constrained smile, "If it were ever to happen that I wished to borrow money, you would not think of this day, and I am not the man then to remind you of it."

"Remind us of it, and you shall see that we will redeem our pledge," said Ephraim. "Come to us and say, 'Remember the hearth-tax from which I got you exempted,' and we will gladly do all and every thing you wish."*

"God grant that I may never have occasion to recal this eventful day to your memory," cried Gotzkowsky, gently repulsing the Jews who thronged round him; and, approaching Tottleben, "Your Excellency," said he, "you have forgotten that you appointed our worthy magistracy to meet you here; these gentlemen are now awaiting your commands."

Tottleben appeared to start from a reverie. "Alas!" said he, in a low voice, "my German dream is dissolved, and I must now be once more a Russian."

He turned to Gotzkowsky, and, with a sudden impulse, stretched out his hand to him: "Gotzkowsky," said he, in a low, impressive voice, "be persuaded—think it over once more—come with me, and be my teacher and friend."

"What I could teach you, General, is little

* Prussia: History of Frederick the Great, vol. ii. p. 254.

indeed," said Gotzkowsky, gently; "easily learned, indeed, by him who has a heart, but impossible for him who has none—learn to love mankind! This is the whole sum of my wisdom, and my last farewell!"

The General sighed deeply. "You will not come with me?" said he sorrowfully, "then farewell!" and at the same moment, as if wishing to disperse the bitter and painful feelings which assailed his heart, he turned suddenly to his aide-de-camp, calling out in the Russian language. "To arms, gentlemen! we must set off. Forward! forward!"

But through the midst of all the confusion, and crowd of soldiers, and stamping horses, the Mayor now made his way. He was resolved to maintain the honour of his fellow magistrates, and also to deliver himself of the fine speech which he had so carefully studied, and which had cost him at least two sleepless nights. He was also bound to give into the hands of the Russian General the sum of money allotted to him by the gratitude of the Berlin people.

At last he succeeded in pushing his way to the General and began his speech. His voice sounded full and clear through the Neumarkt, and the well pleased crowd were delighted by the talent for oratory displayed by their honoured mayor, and looked with pride and admiration at his fine gold chain—this grand and famed gold chain which has seen so much, and survived so much, without turning either pale or dim. But General Tottleben refused to accept the present offered to him by the city. He said, "If the city considers that the good discipline of our soldiers has made its fate less severe, it is to the strict orders of our Empress they owe this boon. I am sufficiently rewarded by having enjoyed the honour of being, during three days, the commandant of Berlin."*

* Gotzkowsky himself relates, "Fourteen days elapsed during which I was loaded with the greatest commendations and encomiums, both from our own city and from foreign countries, of which I still possess the originals, and where I am called by many thousand men their deliverer and benefactor."—Biography of a Patriotic Merchant, page 51.

Three hours afterwards Berlin was free from Russians and Austrians.

Gotzkowsky, who had at length succeeded in extricating himself from the noisy expressions of gratitude of the magistrates, the Jews, and the two editors, returned to his own house, of which he himself said, "My house looked more like a stable than a gentleman's residence, having been occupied day and night by Russians."

---

## BRIDE AND DAUGHTER.

At the intelligence of the approach of the King to Berlin, the Russian army had quitted the city to proceed to Frankfort with all speed; but a considerable number of officers had, nevertheless, remained behind, partly to arrange the order in which the troops were to march, or, detained by their private affairs, they had got a short period of leave.

To the latter category belonged Colonel Féodor von Brenda. General Bachmann had granted him a furlough of two days, imagining that the young colonel would employ his time in the enjoyment of his bride's society, Countess Lodoiska von Sandomir. General Bachmann knew nothing of the coolness between the betrothed; far less that the Countess, in conformity with Bertram's advice, had not even informed Féodor of her arrival in Berlin.

But Féodor was aware of it, nevertheless. The Countess's waiting-woman, knowing from experience the liberality of the young Count, had come to him and betrayed, for a golden reward, the arrival of the Countess, and communicated to him all that by spying and watching she had discovered as to her lady's plans and intentions.

This circumstance had detained Colonel von Brenda in Berlin. The unexpected arrival of his betrothed bride compelled him to come to a decision. He felt the utter impossibility of rending asunder the tender bands which united him to Elise, to fetter himself to a wife to whom his pledged word alone still bound him. Féodor would probably have gladly given up his whole property to discharge his debt of honour; he would have unhesitatingly cast his very life into the scale to redeem his pledge; but he did not scruple to break faith with a loving woman, and to desert her, to whom he had sworn eternal fidelity. In the meantime the unexpected arrival of the Countess had irritated his pride, and appeared to him in the light of a persecution, and an infringement of his liberty. She had concealed her intentions from him, and consequently he imagined that she had been informed of his faithlessness, and had contrived some scheme to overcome the obstacles which separated her from her lover.

His pride, however, revolted from the idea of being forced into a connexion which he could no longer embrace from love, but only from a feeling of duty. Such a limitation of his free will appeared to him a grievous injury. He felt that he actually hated the woman who thus persisted in thrusting herself on him, and was equally devoted to the young girl from whom the Countess wished to separate him.

The young, innocent, attractive Elise appeared doubly amiable and loveable when compared with the brilliant, clever woman of the world, where the best hope he could have was that he was her *last* love, while he knew that he was his Elise's first and only one. His heart filled with these proud and passionate feelings, he went to seek Elise.

But to see her had now become not only

difficult, but almost impossible. Bertram, who, however, had resolved never to betray to Gotzkowsky the forcible abduction of his daughter, had quietly made arrangements which precluded the possibility of a similar enterprise, from whatever source it might proceed, ever being successful.

Under the pretext that the retreat of the enemy's troops made the city unsafe, filling it with marauders and plundering deserters, Bertram, knowing Gotzkowsky's disposition, had armed a number of the workmen and posted them as sentinels round the garden wall, in the court-yard, and in the ground floor of the house itself. They were charged to admit no one who could not give the reason and purpose of his visit. By these precautions Bertram prevented the possibility of Féodor climbing over the garden paling, and also succeeded in preventing Elise, who was embarrassed by the vicinity of the sentinels, from seeking out the more solitary part of the grounds; on the contrary, she now confined herself very much to her own apartments.

In this way Bertram had made a meeting between Féodor and Elise impracticable; but he had not with all his precautions been able to prevent the Count's servant, Petrowitsch, meeting his little love, Elise's waiting-woman, in the street. Through their intervention a letter from Féodor reached Elise; in it he reminded her solemnly and earnestly of the sacred promise she had given; he called on her to fulfil her vow, and to follow him from her father's house. He implored her to unite herself with him at the altar, and thus to give him the right to take her with him to Russia.

Elise had received her lover's letter, and in reading it her heart trembled with mingled emotions.

She scarcely knew whether it was joy or pain which suddenly seized her heart like a spasm, and almost deprived her of consciousness. She felt the most intense delight at the prospect of being at last united to her lover in such sacred bonds, and yet most acute sorrow that the blessing of her father was not to accompany her to the altar; and even the love which spoke so loudly and powerfully in her heart could not drown the warning voice of conscience, that voice which whispered to her of guilt and shame, sin and disgrace.

But Elise strove, in the passionate emotion of her heart, to find an excuse, and in the pride of her injured filial love she said to herself, "My father loves me not; he will not weep for my loss—I am superfluous here—and when I am gone I shall scarcely be missed. He will still have his millions, his friends, and the crowds of those whom he has benefited. He is so rich, he has so much to which he clings!—but I am poor—I have nothing but the heart of my lover—his love is my sole treasure—it would be folly on my part if I rejected this to lead a solitary deserted life, and to fade away unlamented and unmourned. If my father truly loved me, he would not have left me during these days of anxiety and danger. After the dreadful scene in which my heart revolted against his sternness, he should at least have given me an opportunity to implore his forgiveness and pity. He has closed his heart against me; he has absented himself on purpose, and avoids seeing me again. He loves me no longer! I am therefore justified in transferring my devotion to my Féodor. He will never forsake nor forget me, he will always fondly love me, and I feel that I shall ever be his dearest treasure."

While thinking thus, she pressed her lover's letter to her lips, as if each word were written in characters of fire calling on her to perform her vow. All hesitation was at an end. She had at last formed a resolution; and, with flushed cheeks and a palpitating heart, she hastened to her writing table, to express her assent, and to answer Féodor's letter.

"You remind me of my promise," wrote she; "I am ready to fulfil it. Come, then, to lead me from my father's house to the altar, and I will follow you as your wife, and 'whither thou goest I will go.' Your heart shall be henceforth my home; but, while I joyfully accept this home, I banish myself from my father's heart for ever. God will forgive a transgression caused by love so fervid and so pure as ours."

When, however, this letter was actually despatched, when she knew that her lover must have received it, a timid fear, a conscious embarrassment, assailed her. She felt as if a new source of love began to rise in her heart,—as if she had never loved her father so truly or so tenderly as now, when she was about to leave him for ever.

All remorse was now too late,—the decision was made. She could no longer draw back, for she had received a second letter from Féodor, in which he detailed to her the plan for their elopement, and she had given her consent.

All preparations were completed, and now she had nothing more to do but to remain in her room, expecting the appointed signal which was to announce Féodor's arrival.

As soon as she heard it, she was to leave the house with the waiting-maid, who was to accompany her, and to go into the street, where Féodor was to meet her with a carriage, and drive straight to church. There a priest was to meet them, who had been won over by a heavy bribe to perform the ceremony of marriage, thus entitling Féodor to lead his young wife out into the world with him, and rendering it Elise's duty "to leave father and mother, to cleave to her husband."

Some hours were yet to elapse till the arrival of the appointed time. Elise, condemned to the monotony of waiting and expectation, felt all the torture and anxiety which is inevitable at the near approach of a decisive moment of life. She thought of her father with regret and longing, and, though she incessantly repeated to herself that he would never miss her—that he would not mourn her absence—yet her vivid and excitable fancy painted in dreary images his astonishment and anguish, and his anxious search for her.

For the first time she seemed fully to realise that she was about to desert him for ever, without one word of reconciliation, without even having entreated his pardon, or having once more felt a father's kiss on her forehead. She must at least write to him a few words of love and of farewell. She did so, and poured forth on paper all her suppressed tenderness, her anguish, and self-reproach, and this she intended to leave as an olive branch of peace.

When she had written the letter she folded it up, and placed it in her bosom, to take it unobserved to her father's room. He was not there; for two days past he had scarcely been in his own house. She could therefore venture to go to his apartment without the fear of meeting him. She felt that she could not have borne the sight of his kindly face, or the glance of his full, piercing eye.

Slowly and cautiously, in secret terror lest she should meet Bertram on her way to her father's room, whose sad and reproachful looks she dreaded almost more than her father's eye, she glided along the corridor, and at last, panting and breathless, reached the ante-room, without having seen any one. All was still and solitary here.

Her father had not yet returned, and she was quite certain not to be surprised by him. She went into his room, and, traversing it quickly, she was about to open a desk on his writing table to place her letter in it, when she suddenly heard the door of the ante-room open.

She had only time to hide the letter again within the folds of her dress; flight was impossible. It was her father who entered the room. Both, startled by this unexpected encounter, stood speechless and motionless; each hoping that the other would utter some words of greeting and conciliation.

But, however loudly their hearts spoke to each other, their lips remained dumb, and their glances avoided meeting.

"She is afraid of me! This is my welcome after so many weary and toilsome days of absence," thought Gotzkowsky, in grief and sorrow.

"He will not look round—he avoids turning his eyes on me—he has not therefore yet forgiven me," thought Elise, while glancing with timid anxiety at her father's pale and exhausted appearance. "No; he is resolved not to see me—at least, I will be obedient to his wishes this last time, and leave him."

She advanced towards the door at the other

end of the room, gently and sorrowfully. Gotzkowsky's eyes followed her steps. If she had dared to raise her eyes to his, she would have read in her father's loving glance his tender forgiveness.

But she did not venture to look up, and Gotzkowsky said to himself, in the bitterness of his heart, "What would it avail were I to speak to her—she would only misunderstand me? I will lie down to rest, and try to forget my cares and sorrows. I can say nothing to her at this moment, for I am quite exhausted, and tired to death. I have neither composure nor sufficient self possession, to enable me to explain to her all my love and tenderness."

He looked at her, however, with affectionate anxiety as she slowly drew nearer to the door. She was now on the threshold, and her trembling hand touched the handle of the door, but she hesitated to open it, still hoping and longing for one word from her father, even though it were a reproachful one.

And at last it came. Her father's voice sounded like seraphic music in her ear. He called her name, and, stretching out his hand to her, said, with touching gentleness, "Give me your hand, my darling Elise. Come to me, my child—it is so long since I have seen you!"

She turned towards him, but she had not yet courage to look at him. Seizing his offered hand, she pressed it humbly to her lips. "You remember, then," said she, "that you have been so long absent? You have not entirely forgotten me?"

"I forget you!" cried her father, tenderly; but, as if almost ashamed of this hasty cry of paternal love, he said, with more composure and almost in a stern tone, "I have much to say to you, Elise. You accused me of——"

Elise interrupted him with agitated anxiety.

"I was out of my senses," said she, nervously; "forgive me, father—excitement made me unjust."

"No, it only brought to your lips what you had long secretly cherished in your heart,"—and the remembrance of that unhappy hour made his voice falter, and filled him with deep sorrow.

"You were, for the first time, candid with me. Perhaps I am myself to blame for this, but it grieves me to the heart."

He was silent for a moment, apparently overcome by these painful reminiscences.

Elise said nothing, she only gazed at him, and his pale and worn face touched her feelings, and brought tears to her eyes. Suddenly Gotzkowsky looked up, and his face resumed all its usual energy and resolution.

"Let us discuss this matter some other time," said he sternly; "only let me say one thing at present. I wish in no way to restrain you, and I have never done so. You are free to dispose of all I have, except my good name; this I must preserve inviolate for my own sake. As a man of honour, I cannot incur the disgrace of uniting my daughter to a Russian—a foe to my Fatherland. Select a German husband, and, be he who he may, I will gladly welcome any one whom you love, and even willingly sacrifice for your sake, former plans and wishes, that I have long cherished. But my consent to the union of my only child with a Russian, I never will give so long as I live!"

While he spoke thus both their features assumed a very different and startling expression—obstinacy, anger, and defiance were depicted in their mutual aspect, and the spell was dissolved which love had previously exercised on their feelings. Gotzkowsky was no longer the tender, easily reconciled father, ready to listen to loving words—he was now the indignant patriot, wounded in his most sacred rights, and in his honour. Elise was no more the humble and repentant daughter, but the impassioned bride dreading the loss of her lover.

"You are resolved, then, never to give your consent?" asked she indignantly. "If this war were ended; if Russia were no longer to be the enemy of our native land; if——"

"Russia must ever remain the foe to Germany, even though not opposed to her in open strife," interrupted Gotzkowsky. "It is the animosity of despotic power towards intellect and civilisation. Never can the free German spirit be the friend and brother of the barbarian and slave. No more of this! You now know my determination; I cannot alter it, even if it causes you to doubt my love. True love is often proved more by what it denies, than by what it bestows."

Elise clasped her hands, and murmured some low inaudible words. Gotzkowsky felt that it would be wiser, for the sake of both, to break off this painful conversation, before it again roused them to mutual irritation and bitterness. Moreover, he felt that, after so many days of excitement and exaltation, his wearied frame required repose. He therefore went up to his daughter, and held out his hand to her as a friendly farewell.

Elise seized his hand, and pressed it to her lips with passionate emotion. He turned, and crossed the room to go to his sleeping apartment. Elise looked after him with painful longing, and the further her father went from her, the more her agitation seemed to increase. When he was on the point of opening the door she rushed up to him, and exclaimed in a soft imploring tone, "Father!"

Gotzkowsky felt touched to the heart by this agitated cry. He turned, and stretched out his arms to her. She threw herself on his breast with an exclamation of joy, and rested there for a moment in happy self forgetfulness. They looked at each other with a smile, in token of a loving farewell. Gotzkowsky passed through the door. He was gone; she could no longer see him. Father and daughter were severed. Elise felt the most acute pain in the thought, and remorse quite overpowered her. She knew that she ought not to forsake her father, and that it would be disgraceful in her to steal forth from his house secretly like a criminal, even though it were to follow her lover to the bridal altar. She felt as if she must call her father back, embrace his knees, and entreat him to save her from her own weakness. Already she had unclosed her lips, and stretched out her arms towards the door, when suddenly she trembled, and her arms sunk by her side. She had heard the loud rolling of carriage-wheels, and she knew what this meant. This very equipage, which was now at the door, was in all probability the one in which Féodor had come to fetch her. "It is too late! I can no longer draw back," said she sorrowfully, and she slowly quitted her father's apartments to return to her own.

## THE RIVALS.

Scarcely had Elise reached her room when she hurried to the window and looked down into the street, over which the twilight of evening was already spreading a dusky veil.

She was not mistaken, a carriage was before her door, but, to her surprise, she did not hear the concerted signal, the post-horn sounding the Russian melody of "Schöne Minka;" besides, it was not yet the appointed hour, and her waiting woman, who was watching below on the ground floor, did not appear to summon her.

Elise remained standing at the window, for involuntarily she felt herself alarmed by the arrival of this carriage. Suddenly she heard a violent knocking at her door; before she had time to form any resolution it was hastily opened, and Bertram entered with a thickly veiled lady, leaning on his arm. "Bertram!" exclaimed Elise, timidly, "what do you want here?" "I will tell you," said Bertram, gravely, "I am come to ask a favour from my sister. I have pledged myself to this lady, that she should have an opportunity of seeing and speaking to you. I hope you will redeem my pledge."

"What does the lady wish to say to me?" asked Elise, casting a timid, frightened glance at the mysterious figure.

"She will herself inform you of her wishes. She entreated me, with tears, to take her to Elise Gotzkowsky, assuring me that the happiness of her whole life depended on her seeing you." Elise felt that a dreadful overwhelming shock threatened her, and she began visibly to tremble, and to shrink from the veiled lady. She pressed her hand to her heart, as if wishing to shield it from the deadly peril which a presentiment made her feel was drawing near; and she murmured, with quivering lips, "What does this stranger wish?"

Bertram did not answer, but dropped the arm of the unknown lady and bowed. "Countess!" said he, "this is Mademoiselle Elise

Gotzkowsky. I have fulfilled my promise. You must, therefore, permit me to leave you, and may a higher power endow your words with all the strength of full conviction!" He greeted the two ladies respectfully and left the room.

"You wished to speak to me," said Elise, at last, in a faltering, suppressed voice. "May I entreat ——"

The lady threw back her veil hurriedly, displaying a lovely face, covered with tears. "It is I who must entreat," said she, in a touching voice, and with a foreign accent, and seizing Elise's hand, she pressed it warmly to her heart, and continued. "Pardon me! Now that I see you I no longer remember what I intended to say. All my entreaties, all my indignant feelings, have vanished at sight of you. You are very beautiful! Be as noble-minded as you are fair. It is in your power to make me happy—to restore felicity to me!"

"God alone can do that," said Elise, solemnly.

"At this moment you represent the fate

which must decide my happiness or never-ending misery," exclaimed the Countess. "You alone can restore to me the bliss of which you have deprived me. Yes; you, with all your youth, beauty, and innocence, are the destroyer of my happiness."

Her eyes sparkled, and a feverish flush rose to her pallid cheeks. "Ah!" continued she, more vehemently, "I have now overcome my embarrassment, and anger is again my prevalent feeling. I am once more the lioness struggling for her life and her love."

Elise drew herself up to her full height, for she also felt a transformation in her heart. She knew, with the instinct of a loving soul, that the beautiful creature who stood opposite to her, with scornful and threatening aspect, was her enemy and her rival. Glowing wrath filled her whole soul, and she mentally vowed not to give way a hair's breadth, or to shrink from this proud beauty.

She fixed her eyes with scornful pride on the Countess. Their angry glances crossed, like the glittering points of two swords in a duel.

"I do not comprehend you," said Elise, with contemptuous coolness. "You must speak more plainly, if you wish me to understand you!"

"You do not choose to understand me," cried the Countess. "You wish to evade my entreaties, but that cannot be. I have suffered so much that I am resolved to suffer no more; we stand here, at this moment, two women, who must do deadly battle together for life or death."

Elise suppressed the cry of anguish which rose to her lips, and imposed on herself the appearance of proud calmness. "I certainly do not understand you," said she coldly; "and I have no desire whatever to enter into any disagreeable discussion with a lady who is an entire stranger to me. If you therefore are resolved not to leave this room, permit me to do so."

She turned to go, but the Countess eagerly seized her hand to detain her. "No, you must not, you shall not leave me," cried she passionately; "you shall not go, for I know you would go to him—to *him* whom I love; and I am come to demand back from you the man I idolise."

These threatening and imperious words at length roused Elise from her assumed composure, and she said indignantly, "I don't know of whom you are speaking."

But the Countess was weary of hints and inuendoes: "You know well," cried she angrily; "you know that I come hither solely to recover my most sacred treasure—the heart of my lover—from you. Oh! be merciful, and give me back my Féodor—for he is mine, and mine alone. Have compassion on my tears. You are so young, so rich, so lovely—you have all that can make life happy; I have nothing but *him*. Leave him to me."

Elise felt as if a paroxysm of despair had seized her—as if she could spring like a tigress at the woman who came to deprive her of her lover. With a wild scornful laugh she said, "You say that you love him? then go to him and ask him to give you back his heart. Why do you seek it from me? Reconquer it from himself, if you have the power."

"If I am to do so," cried the Countess, "you must first release him from the fetters with which you have enchained him."

Elise's pale cheeks became crimson: "You are insolent," said she.

The Countess did not seem to heed her anger, but continued: "Set him free; if you will only loosen the links which bind him to you, I know he will again return to me."

Elise looked earnestly at the Countess, whose face was now bathed in tears. She had only heard one solitary word; but this one word had stabbed her to the heart. "*Again* return to you?" asked she breathlessly; "was he once yours?"

"I withheld nothing from him—everything I treasured on earth I flung at his feet," exclaimed the Countess sadly.

Elise uttered a cry of misery, and buried her face in her hands. Her agitation was so great and so distressing, that it even moved the heart of her rival to sympathy. With evident compassion she placed her hand gently on Elise's arm, and led her to a sofa. "Come," said she, "let us converse like two sisters; only listen to me patiently, and I will unfold a true picture which will make you shudder."

Elise yielded to the Countess's impulse, and mechanically followed her to the couch, allowing her rival to retain her hand. "Féodor was hers," murmured she; "he once gave his heart to another!"

"Will you hear me?" asked the Countess; and, seeing that Elise had fixed her eyes on the ground in a gloomy reverie, she cried, "I will relate to you the sad story of my betrothed, and of his unhappy forsaken bride."

Elise started, and looked at her with the bewildered glance of despair. "Speak," said she in a faltering voice; "and I will listen."

Countess Lodoiska von Sandomir related to the young girl—often interrupted by her sobs and sighs of sympathy—the sad and painful tale of her love and of her desertion. She told her of her solemn betrothal to her lover, in the presence of the Empress herself. The day of her wedding was even finally fixed; but a few short weeks previous to that period war broke out, and her lover, at the call of honour and duty, resolved to accompany his regiment on service. He had sworn never to forget her, and ever to remain faithful to her, and she had believed him.

The Countess fixed her large melancholy eyes on the young girl, who, pale and absorbed in her grief, sat like a statue, and said, "I have not yet told you the name of my lover—is it necessary for me to do so?"

Elise started up, as if roused from an evil dream: "No!" said she in a tone of anguish, "do not name him; what have I to do with him? I know him not. I will not hear it. The name of such a traitor cannot concern me."

"You must hear it," said Lodoiska sternly; "it is Féodor von Brenda."

Elise uttered a cry of misery, and sunk back half insensible on the sofa; but this state of unconsciousness did not last long.

Her heart, which had for a moment seemed to cease to beat under the pressure of this violent shock, began once more to palpitate with violence; the blood rushed through her veins with double impulse; and her soul, not yet inured to the weight of hopeless grief, made a last effort to free itself from the fetters which oppressed her. Her cheeks glowed, and her eyes were bright from feverish agitation, while she vehemently exclaimed, "It is false—a miserable invention to separate me from Féodor! Ah! now I see it all; I understand my father's solemn assurances, and why Bertram brought you hither—but you are much mistaken in your estimate of me. Away! Countess! and say to those who sent you, that Elise sacrifices all to him whom she loves, and in whose honour she places implicit faith, even though the whole world should testify against him."

And with a haughty air and scornful smile she rose to leave the room. The Countess, looking at her with pity, said, "You will not, then, believe me? will you believe this testimony?"

She took a letter from her bosom, and gave it to Elise.

"It is Féodor's writing," exclaimed the

young girl, with a start, eagerly seizing the letter.

"Ah! you know his writing? he has written to you, also, the traitor," sighed the Countess. "Read it—it is a letter which he wrote to me at the beginning of his captivity in Berlin—read it."

"I will read it," said Elise, faintly; "these well-known characters are like daggers to me; but I will take courage, and know the worst." Slowly, and with wonderful composure, she perused the letter which destroyed her happiness for ever.

The poison of those words of endearment addressed to another fell drop by drop into her soul; those assurances of never dying fidelity and passionate love! She gazed long and searchingly at the signature, as if wishing to convince herself of its reality, and then, restoring the letter to the countess, she murmured, half unconsciously, "Heavens! how fondly I loved that man!" and, no longer able to restrain her agitation, she burst into tears, and, hiding her face in her hands, sobbed aloud in unrestrained misery.

"Poor unhappy girl!" cried the Countess, placing her hand gently on Elise's arm.

Elise started back and looked at her indignantly, "Do not pity me," said she, "I do not want your compassion; I——" Suddenly she broke off, and an electric shudder seemed to convulse her frame—she had heard the preconcerted signal, the tones of the post horn, which clearly and slowly rung forth the melancholy Russian melody, sounding, now, to Elise, like her final doom; at last the notes died away, and a well known, and still much loved voice, called, softly, "Elise, Elise!"

The young girl started and shuddered. "I shrink from his voice," said she; yet she could not resist the impulse to respond to the call, for she went to the window, though with faltering steps, and looked out below.

Countess Lodoiska watched her with a jealous eye, and a fearful thought suddenly assailed her. What if this young girl loved Féodor as fondly as she did! What if she were ready to forgive the past, and to efface with the hand of love his treachery; to commence a new existence with him! What if she were to feel no sympathy with Féodor's deserted bride, but prepared triumphantly to trample on her heart, to follow the steps of her lover, and to accompany him to the altar?

A feeling of despair paralysed her heart.

"Fly with him!" said she, with a mocking laugh; "desert your father, whose confidence you betray for the sake of a traitor; you have sworn to love him—go to him and fulfil your vow."

Féodor's voice was again heard calling more earnestly and loudly on Elise's name.

She stood for a few moments listening, and then rushing to the window she threw it open, calling out "I come, I come."

But Lodoiska seized her arm, and drew her away with no gentle hand, exclaiming breathlessly, "Traitress, you shall not cross this threshold—I will appeal to your father—I will call the whole household together."

"You will call no one," interrupted Elise, and her proud, cool composure made an impression even on her agitated rival. "You shall not require to call for the aid of any one, for I remain here, and you—you shall go in my place."

"What do you say?" asked Lodoiska.

Elise raised her hand and pointed to the window. "I say," said she, "that your betrothed awaits you yonder—go to him, in God's name!"

The Countess threw her arms round Elise's neck with a cry of joy—"You renounce him, then?"

"I have no more interest in his fate or claim on his love," said Elise, coldly. "He is yours—go to him."

The Countess looked at her, and hesitated; but Elise repeated, more vehemently, "Go to him at once—hasten—he is waiting for you!"

"But he will recognise me, and repulse me," said Lodoiska, sadly.

Elise pointed to her travelling-dress, which was on a sofa. "Take these things," said she, imperiously; "my bonnet and cloak will disguise you sufficiently. Keep the thick veil down. He knows the dress, and will not for an instant have any suspicion."

At this moment the door was impetuously thrown open, and Bertram looked in. "Make haste," cried he, "or all is lost. Count Féodor is out of patience, and he will probably venture even to come up here in search of Elise. Gotzkowsky, too, has been awakened by the unusual sound of the post-horn."

"Assist the Countess to prepare for her journey, Bertram," said Elise, who was still standing motionless and rigid.

Bertram looked at her in astonishment; but the Countess, in a few hurried words, explained to him Elise's purpose, and her intention that she should assume her travelling dress, and accompany Féodor in her place.

Bertram gave one of those glances at Elise in which the whole soul of a man is condensed. He felt the deepest admiration of the young creature, thus capable of heroically vanquishing her own feelings, from a sense of honour. He had placed reliance on her maidenly pride, her rectitude, and her justice, and he had not been deceived.

The Countess had hastily thrown on Elise's travelling attire. Bertram entreated her to make all possible haste, and Lodoiska turned hurriedly to Elise to take leave of her, and to thank her warmly for the sacrifice she had made for her sake.

But Elise repulsed her coldly and proudly, and seemed secretly to shudder at her emotion. "Rejoin your betrothed, Countess!" said she, and her voice sounded loud and harsh.

Lodoiska's eyes filled with tears. She tried once more to clasp Elise's hand; but she folded her arms, and looked at her sternly. "Go! pray go at once," said she resolutely.

Bertram seized the Countess's arm, and hurried her to the door. "Make haste! You have not a moment to lose!"

The door closed behind them—Elise was alone.

She stood and listened to their retreating steps, she heard the house door open, and the post-horn gaily resume its melody, the wheels of the carriage roll along, and the tones of "Schöne Minka" gradually die away in the distance.

"I am alone!" said she, with a cry of anguish. "They are gone together—I am alone!"

She raised her hands to heaven in despairing misery, and cried in anguish, "Will no one have compassion on me?—will no one look on me with pity?"

"Elise!" said her father, opening the door of her room.

She sprang towards him with a loud cry, and, clinging to him and resting her head on his breast, she said faintly, "Have pity on me, father—do not repulse me! You are my sole refuge—my sole happiness in this world."

Gotzkowsky pressed her fondly to his heart, and turned his eyes to heaven in deep thankfulness.

"Ah!" said he, softly, "I knew my darling's heart would soon turn again to her father." He tenderly kissed her glossy hair, and the fair face resting on his breast.

"Weep not, my child, weep not," whispered he.

"Let me weep," said she, in a weary tone. "You little know how much grief and remorse these tears wash away. Press me closer to your heart. I am alone and forsaken in this world!"

The door opened once more and Bertram came in hastily.

"He did not recognise her, and they are gone——" suddenly he stopped at sight of Gotzkowsky, whose presence he had not at first perceived. Gotzkowsky asked, in surprise, "Who is gone? what does all this mean?"

Elise extricated herself from his arms and looked at him with sparkling eyes, and flushed cheeks.

"It means," said she, "that all happiness in this life is at an end for me—that all is false and deceptive—love, faith, and happiness!" and with a piercing cry, she fell back into her father's arms.

"Do not try to restore her yet, father," said Bertram, bending over her. "Grant her this short moment of respite from misery; she has a great sorrow to overcome; when she recovers consciousness, she will love no one so dearly as her father."

Gotzkowsky pressed his lips to her forehead, and inwardly invoked a blessing on her head.

"She shall henceforth find a loving father in me," said he, deeply moved, "who will even weep with her if such sympathy is any consolation—a father may well lament with such a daughter!"

## THE FÊTE OF GRATITUDE.

Berlin had at last in some degree recovered from the sad misery it had suffered. The enemy had left the city eight days, and all was again still and peaceful.

But on this day the calm was to be interrupted by a gay and joyful festival. Berlin, after having endured so much, purposed on this particular day once more to rejoice.

The occasion of this festivity was none other than the wish to do honour to Johann Gotzkowsky, the Merchant Patriot of Berlin, the man whom the whole of Berlin considered a guardian angel and protector. He had joyfully borne anxiety and discomfort, danger and fatigue, for the sake of his fellow citizens. They had always found him kind and unselfish, and willing to oblige and serve them. The whole city felt that they were his debtors; he had done good service to every class of society, and therefore they all wished to testify their gratitude.

Gotzkowsky had been requested not to leave his house on the morning of the important day, but to be prepared to receive some deputations, to be followed by a solemn banquet which the citizens of Berlin had commanded in honour of their hero. They were to eat and drink, to shout and rejoice, all in honour of Gotzkowsky; his health was to be given with loud cheers, and drunk in champagne by the whole assemblage; it was expected that Gotzkowsky would consider it a very grand festival, and given entirely in his honour. He had in vain endeavoured to decline this banquet: he at first attempted to escape from it on the plea that his daughter was ill, and that he could not leave her sick bed; but they had taken information from the physician, who had assured them that Elise was now quite out of danger, and that her father could perfectly well leave her for a few hours without any feelings of anxiety or uneasiness. Gotzkowsky could devise no other excuse to withdraw from this festival; he was therefore obliged to declare his readiness to accept it.

Elise was in truth very ill—she had sunk under the sorrow and misery of her betrayed and loving heart, and her despairing lamentations, the reproaches she uttered during her delirium, in imaginary conversations with her lover, had betrayed to her father the secrets of her poor suffering heart. He thanked God in deep emotion for her escape, and had no feeling of anger against his unhappy, misled child, who, in the solitude of her own heart, had sought refuge in this love, as in a sheltering haven.

But he bitterly reproached himself, and in the depths of his remorse he mentally said, "Elise has a right to doubt my fatherly love and tenderness—I endured my loneliness, and constant separation from my daughter, because I thought I was engaged in her service, and therefore gladly, for her sake, sacrificed myself; but I forgot that she also was dull and solitary, that she missed a father's care as much as I did the love of my child—I strove to make her rich, and I have only made her poor and wretched."

He kissed Elise's burning fevered forehead, and with tears cordially pardoned in his inmost heart the aberrations which an unhappy passion had caused. She was still with him—she had sought refuge in his arms; in her despair she had appealed to her father's heart, imploring his aid and sympathy.

Gloomy clouds had now passed away, and the sky was again bright and clear—Berlin was freed from its foes. Elise was rapidly recovering, and the city had prepared a grand banquet in honour of their noblest citizen.

The hour appointed for Gotzkowsky to receive the deputation had arrived, and he went into the large hall overlooking the garden. Thundering cheers welcomed him—they came from his workmen who had just entered the garden, and were waving their hats and caps, followed by a crowd of women dressed in mourning; they had for this day suppressed their grief and tears for their sons and husbands fallen in battle, and came to thank Gotzkowsky with grateful smiles for the noble manner in which he had adopted them, and provided for their families. Behind the women were many poor orphans with crape round their arms; they came along merrily stretching out their little hands to their benefactor, and at the word of command, given by Balthazar their leader, they with one accord uttered so shrill a shout that the windows rattled.

"One cheer more!" cried the enthusiastic Balthazar.

Children and workmen all once more united in one hearty cheer. Gotzkowsky said, laughing, and seizing Balthazar's arm, "For Heaven's sake make less noise; don't you know that I must have the full use of my ears to-day? Your shouting will utterly deafen me: enough, enough!"

Balthazar extricated himself, struggling from his master's grasp, and placed himself opposite to him. He could indulge in his love of speaking to-day, for his fellow workmen had appointed him their spokesman on this occasion. He was therefore justified in holding forth.

When he commenced, his beaming eyes and warm heartfelt enthusiasm proved that his words were not studied, but flowed direct from his heart. "Let them cheer and shout, sir," said he, "for it is indeed a cause for thankfulness to possess such a master. Look at these children! a few days since they had fathers to work for them, and to care for them. They have been deprived of them by cannon balls; but God has given them a new father, and that father is yourself. You adopted these children when forsaken by all the world beside. You said, 'Providence has doomed these poor children to become orphans, their brave fathers having fallen in the fight for freedom; I will be their father.' Ask the widows for whom they pray to God?—ask the poor who were starving, and whom you fed—ask the whole city, who it is they most prize and love? They will all utter the name of Gotzkowsky—they will shout with one accord, 'Long live our father and our friend!'"

Once more a unanimous shout was heard confirming these sentiments.

Gotzkowsky, deeply moved, shook hands cordially with his workpeople, and accepted with a grateful smile the flowers the children had brought him.

"I thank you—I thank you!" said he, with emotion; "you have richly rewarded me, for I see that you loveme,—and what gift in this world is so precious as love?"

"Diamonds!" cried Ephraim, emphatically, making his way through the crowd with Itzig and a deputation from the Jewish community to the hero of the day: "I say that diamonds are infinitely more precious than love. Look, Gotzkowsky, here is a brilliant which flames and sparkles more brightly than the most loving glances of man or woman ever did."

He held up a valuable solitaire diamond to Gotzkowsky, and continued, "Be so good as to do us the favour to accept this gift from our grateful community; it is a gem of purest water."

"It is a crystallized tear of joy," interrupted Itzig, "shed at the joyful tidings that you had succeeded in getting us exempted from the hearth tax. You are our great benefactor—our best friend. You have been, indeed, the Providence of the Jews in these troubled times, and preserved for us what forms the honour, and distinction, and happiness, of every Jew—you have saved our money. A Jew with no money is no man! Take the ring, and wear it in remembrance of us!"

"Take it, we beg," cried Ephraim and all his companions.

Gotzkowsky took the ring, and placing it on his finger, thanked the givers for the costly gift.

Itzig's countenance was overcast, and, while drawing back with Ephraim and his friends, he muttered in a low spiteful tone, "I declare he has taken it! I hoped his pride would induce him to decline it, for it cost a vast sum of money, which we could have employed otherwise very profitably."

The pompous procession of the Berlin magistracy which now appeared interrupted Itzig's private lamentations, and attracted his attention to the Mayor, Herr von Kircheisen, who, in all the pride and dignity of his important office, accompanied by the senators and city officials, came waddling along through the crowd, stretching out his hand cordially to Gotzkowsky, who advanced to meet him.

"The magistrates of Berlin are come to thank you," said he, "for it is a fact quite unexampled that any individual should suffer and sacrifice what you have done, without the slightest self-interest or hope of reward, simply from the wish to serve your fellow citizens."*

"You esteem me more than I deserve," said Gotzkowsky, smiling, when Kircheisen paused. "I had a recompense in view. I wished to gain the love of my fellow townsmen. If I have succeeded in that endeavour I am richly rewarded, and I beg you will say no more on the subject.

The Mayor majestically shook his head.

"You have shown us the virtue of love," said he; "permit us to show you the virtue of gratitude."

* The Mayor's own words. *Vide* Biography of a Patriotic Merchant, p. 136.

He took from the hand of the second burgomaster a dark red velvet casket, containing a beautifully chiselled silver wreath of oak leaves, and presented it to Gotzkowsky.

"Johann Gotzkowsky," said he solemnly, "the magistrates and burghers of Berlin entreat you through me to accept this memento of their love and gratitude. It is the Burgher Crown, which your noble conduct so richly merits. Take it from our hands, and also our vow, that we can never, so long as we live, forget what you have done for this city."

Tears of joy and sincere gratification stood in Gotzkowsky's eyes when he took the silver wreath from the Mayor's hands, and ardent words of gratitude flowed from his lips.

Not far from him Herr Krause and Herr Kretschmer were standing in the recess of a window, looking with a grudging envious eye at the homage paid to Gotzkowsky, which filled their hearts with spite and malice. They had also come to thank him; but they had done so very reluctantly, and only because they could find no excuse for absenting themselves from the fête, which was a testimony of esteem from the whole city.

They were furious to see the man whom they hated in their hearts thus honoured; they detested him the more because they were so deeply indebted to him; they were piqued to see the usually insolent and haughty Mayor address Gotzkowsky with such a gracious smile and with so much respect, and furious at the heartfelt sympathy shown towards him by the counsellors and senators, and all the working classes.

"I came here," said Krause, in a whisper to his ally Kretschmer, "on purpose to thank Gotzkowsky, because he saved us from a barbarous punishment, but I own it does annoy me to see him made such a fuss with."

Kretschmer shrugged his shoulders disdainfully—

"Let them praise him up to the skies, if they like," said he; "the Voss paper shall take no notice of it, and I will not publish the smallest article on this solemnity. As to the service he did us, it would certainly have been vastly disagreeable to have been flogged; but in that case we should have been considered celebrated martyrs in the cause of liberalism, all the world would have admired and pitied us, and the King could not possibly have refused us a pension."

"Certainly not," continued Krause; "honours would have been showered down on us. That English poet, Prynne, whose ears were cut off by order of Charles the First, because he had written libels against His Majesty, was never forgotten. He became famous, not from his poetry, but from the loss of his ears. We might have been equally celebrated if this Gotzkowsky had not interfered in the most uncalled for manner, and —— but see," said he, interrupting himself, "the conversation between him and the magistrates is at an end, and now it is our turn to come forward and thank him.

The two editors hastened up to Gotzkowsky to assure him of their everlasting gratitude, in a set poetical speech and well chosen terms.

## A ROYAL LETTER.

Herr Krause had not yet ended declaiming the poem he had composed in honour of this grand occasion, and of the great Gotzkowsky, when a loud voice was heard at the door of the saloon, and Gotzkowsky's valet hurriedly entered. He said that a King's messenger was without, charged with a letter from His Majesty; and as his orders were to deliver it into the Mayor's own hands he had followed him hither. He gave a letter accordingly to Herr von Kircheisen, who broke the seal with majestic composure.

An anxious silence ensued.

Each asked himself with a beating heart what this missive from the King to the Mayor contained? The countenance of the Mayor brightened visibly more and more, and suddenly he exclaimed, "Here is joyful news for our poor town! The King, our gracious master, releases us from the obligation to pay up the promised war contribution of a million and a half. He will exercise reprisals, on ac- acount of the bonds which are due, and still unliquidated, by the States of Wurtzburg and Bamberg. His Majesty, therefore, commands that we should not pay."*

One universal acclamation of joy burst from the lips of all present. Gotzkowsky alone was silent, and cast down his eyes, his grave and thoughtful mien very little harmonising with the bright smiling faces of the assemblage, who were overwhelmed with delight at the command of the King to keep their money.

Most overjoyed of all, were the rich Jews Ephraim and Itzig, and also the mayor.

"This royal edict relieves our poor city from a fearful burden," said Kircheisen with a happy smile.

"The whole guild of merchants must thank the King," cried Ephraim. "Berlin keeps her

* Russia: History of Frederick the Great, vol. ii. page 251.

million and a half, and our enemies are defrauded."

Gotzkowsky suddenly raised himself from his reverie, his eagle eye measuring the whole assemblage with a bold and fiery glance. "Russia is not defrauded," cried he; "for Berlin will undoubtedly pay the million and a half yet due to her foe. Berlin has promised to do so, and that promise must be kept."

All faces quickly became dark at these bold words, and here and there an exclamation of anger or surprise was heard.

"What!" cried Itzig in a shrill tone, "do you mean that the merchants should throw away such an enormous sum of money, when they can keep it in their pockets? The King himself has said we shall not pay."

"And I say we shall pay," cried Gotzkowsky. "What is written is written; what is promised must be fulfilled, for our honour demands that it should. No king possesses the power to absolve from a promise, or to recal a vow. He who does not keep his word of honour is no honourable man, even if a king."

"But there are certain cases," said Kircheisen soothingly; "cases where the performance of a promise is impossible."

Gotzkowsky answered vehemently: "If there are such, a man of honour must die with his word still unfulfilled; but you have no thoughts of dying; on the contrary, it is your intention to become false to your word to enable you to live all the better. You wish to profit by your faithlessness, to declare yourselves bankrupts, and to defraud your creditors of their money, that you may become rich yourselves."

An unanimous storm of opposition interrupted Gotzkowsky; and those very men who had come expressly to prepare a banquet for him, in token of their gratitude, thronged round him now with angry and threatening gestures.

"A million and a half is no child's play," cried Ephraim. "Money is far more valuable than honour!"

"I say that money *is* honour," croaked Itzig: "when we keep our millions, we keep our honour too!"

"You are very high-minded!" said Kretschmer to Gotzkowsky with a sneer; "you pay like a cavalier from the pockets of others; and, that you may not be accused of any breach of promise, the citizens are to pay a million and a half."

Gotzkowsky cast a glance of contemptuous pity on him. "You forget, sir," said he coolly, "that I negotiated not in my own name, but in that of the magistrates and merchants. It is not I personally who will be alone dishonoured, but the whole city of Berlin."

"But I repeat," cried Kircheisen, "the King desires us not to pay."

"No King has power to do so," interrupted Gotzkowsky impatiently. "A man of honour must keep his word, and no Sovereign on earth has power to release him from such an obligation."

"Do not let us discuss opinions," said Kircheisen. "My advice decidedly is, that we should not pay this million and a half."

"No, no, we will not," cried all present, in great excitement, pressing round the Mayor and detailing in joyful conversation all the advantages which would accrue to each from refusing to pay.

Gotzkowsky stood alone, unobserved and forgotten, listening to them. He felt the deepest depression, the greatest humiliation, and said sorrowfully to himself: "Here is another proof of the unhappy power of gold to harden the heart, and to render it deaf to the call of honour. For the sake of a million and a half of miserable dollars these men are ready and anxious to sacrifice their honour; but I will make one last effort—I will attack them by their cowardice."

He turned once more to them, and with persuasive words and burning eloquence depicted the dangers they would inevitably incur if they refused to pay the bonds they had given. The Russians were as yet not very distant from Berlin—they had retreated by forced marches, but could equally return in the same way, to take revenge in their wrath and fury on the faithless city. "One unlucky moment," said he, "can make the Russians conquerors of our King, and the enemy will in that event return, and tear us to pieces like tigers. I shall then have no more power to protect you, for on me especially, who became a guarantee for the payment of the war contribution by the citizens, will the rage of General Tottleben fall. God himself never protects traitors."

A profound silence ensued when Gotzkowsky ceased speaking. All faces were again overcast, and the gloomy knit brows and anxious aspect of each countenance showed that Gotzkowsky's words had carried conviction to every heart, and converted them to the painful opinion that it was absolutely necessary to liquidate the bonds they had granted.

Even Kircheisen forgot, in his terror at the possible return of the Russians, the amount of the sums to be paid, and said, with a heavy sigh, "I fear, alas! that Gotzkowsky is right. It is bad to pay down money, but worse still to incur on this occasion the risk of not doing so."

"It might cost us our heads," said the second magistrate. Ephraim stood in a dejected attitude and muttered, "Money is dear, but life is dearer still."

Itzig, however, cried in despair, "We will not pay—we will keep our money—the Jew that has no money is no man."

But Kircheisen, who had consulted with the other magistrates in all haste, went up to Gotzkowsky, saying, "We thank you; for you have spoken wisely—we will redeem our bonds, as we cannot do otherwise with safety; but you must do us one more important service, you must go to the King, and entreat him not to be angry with us because we do not intend to obey his royal commands."

"Do so, Gotzkowsky—do so, we beg!" cried all the others; "go to the King—you stand high in his favour—plead for us!"

Gotzkowsky's face beamed with noble satisfaction. "Well," said he, "I will go to the King; I will entreat him to permit the city of Berlin to preserve her honour immaculate, and to pay the promised million and a half."

"Use all your eloquence," said Kircheisen, impressively, "that our Sovereign may remain well disposed towards Berlin, and not visit on us our disobedience of his commands."

"The King is a noble high-hearted man," said Gotzkowsky, with enthusiasm; "his word of honour is sacred to him, and he will enter into our feelings, and esteem us the more that we refuse to break our pledged word."

One hour later, the most distinguished of the magistrates, citizens, and merchants of Berlin repaired to the great Town Hall, where a splendid banquet was prepared; shouts of enthusiasm resounded, toasts were given, there was universal joy and rejoicing, and Berlin celebrated a day of happiness.

The man, however, who was the hero of this feast, whom Berlin named her Saviour and Benefactor, Johann Gotzkowsky, was not present at the banquet, though given expressly in his honour. Wrapped closely in furs, he had just got into his travelling carriage, and, despising fatigue and danger, had driven out in the cold night air towards Meissen, where the King had fixed his quarters.

## FREDERICK THE GREAT AT MEISSEN.

The great battle of Torgau was fought; and, after so much hard fighting and so many bloody victories, the Prussian army was resting from its struggles, and dreaming with secret delight of the winter quarters which it expected to find in Saxony. The head quarters at present were at Meissen, and the King himself was enjoying a few days of repose in the palace there—a King who had for many years past only experienced the anxieties and dangers of power and greatness—a King who often struggled with care and hunger, with daily privations, and peril of death; and who one day, exhausted by sleeping so many nights on the cold ground, begged his aide-de-camp to desire a bundle of straw to be brought into the camp at night for his use.

Frederick the Great had long spared Saxony, for he grieved over this fair and oppressed land;* but he was at last driven to treat it as an inimical country, as his mildness and forbearance had no effect on the Saxons, who seemed to cling with redoubled zeal to the enemies of Prussia.

Soon its trampled corn fields, its silent manufactories, its impoverished towns, and its deserted villages, showed in all their horrors the devastations and miseries of war.

At this moment, however, the opposing camps were quiet and peaceful. Both parties were too exhausted to venture to risk a new battle, and both sides required a little rest and time, after the mutual strain on their strength. Moreover, winter had set in early with unusual severity, and effectually put a stop to the

* In a letter to Algarotti, dated from Freiberg, March 10th, 1760, the King writes: "Cette campagne vient d'abimer la Saxe. J'avais menagé ce beau pays, autant que la fortune me l'avait permis; mais à present la desolation est partout, et, sans parler du mal moral que cette guerre pourra faire, le mal physique ne sera pas la moindre, et nous l'échapperons bien si la peste ne s'ensuit pas."

campaign of 1760. The point of strife now was for winter quarters; and, therefore, after the battle of Torgau the King's first efforts had been directed to cut off the retreat of the Austrians to Dresden, or, at all events, to drive them out of that city. "But they laughed at us from the summits of their mountains," writes Frederick to Gräfin Camas. "I marched back on the spot, and, like a sulky schoolboy, hid myself and my rage in a confounded Saxon village. I assure you I lead the life of a dog, such as no man, except Don Quixote, ever led before me."

In the meantime Frederick had quitted this "confounded Saxon village" (Neustadt), and had gone to Meissen, where, instead of the "life of a dog," a degree of comfort and rest had been substituted.

King Frederick had therefore laid aside his sword for some quiet weeks, and the great Commander in the field had been transformed once more into the Royal poet and philosopher, who shared his time between music and poetry, serious studies and letters to his friends, in which the sublime and lofty thoughts of his enlightened and unprejudiced mind, were displayed in all their strength and beauty.

The King was alone in his study. He had just finished a letter to the Marquis D'Argens, requesting him to give him tidings of his gallery at Sans Souci, and to tell him what progress it had made.

Frederick laid down his pen and leant back in his chair. His usually quick and piercing eye had now a mild and peaceful expression, and a gentle smile played round his thin, compressed, but well chiselled lips. He had for a moment forgotten the turmoil of war and all his cares, and dreamt that he was again in his beloved paradise, Sans Souci—where the hero was permitted once more to be a poet, and where the Monarch could divest himself of his purple for some enjoyable hours, and instead of the despotic ruler and Sovereign become the smiling son of the Muses.

Softened by these reminiscences of happier days, he rose and took up his flute, which, at his particular desire, always lay on his writing-table. He placed it to his lips, and began to play an adagio, in the execution of which he was acknowledged to be one of the greatest virtuosi of his day. The volume of tone ascended and melodiously floated on the air, surrounding him with magic harmony. No one could hear the noble and touching music of the Royal artist without being moved in his inmost soul, and feeling his heart beat with soft emotion.

In the ante-chamber was a group of stern generals and heroic warriors. Ziethen was there, and the valiant Schwerin, and General von Saldern; and their scarred, rugged features had a softened expression, as leaning against the wall they listened in breathless silence to their King's melodious tones.

But these tones suddenly ceased. The brave but unskilful warriors had thought the music sublime, but the King was by no means satisfied with his own playing. Remembering the royal perfection of tone when at Sans Souci, he required of the wandering Monarch, the victim of anxiety and discomfort, the same fullness of melody, the same power and energy of execution. He was annoyed that these tones did not come forth with all the clearness and purity of former days, and he could not endure hearing the sharp sound of his own breathing on the instrument, which accompanied the music like sighs. He threw aside his flute discontentedly, and went up to a mirror. It was seldom, indeed, that the King thought it worth while to examine his personal appearance, and when he did so, it was invariably to trace out some blemish, or sign of decay.

While, therefore, he was gazing at his own image, there was a melancholy expression on his countenance, and he knit his brows gloomily.

What was it which annoyed the valiant hero, the victorious Monarch?

He had perceived that one of his front teeth was chipped, and the gap caused by this accident was the natural explanation of his imperfect playing.

He quitted the glass with an impatient gesture, and began to pace the room with a wrinkled brow and hasty steps; but suddenly his features assumed another expression, and a sarcastic smile played round his mouth

He went to the writing table again on which a quantity of half finished letters were lying, and, selecting from among them one he had been writing to Gräfin Camas, he said to himself, "The good Gräfin has not inquired about my personal appearance; well, I am quite in a mood to draw my own portrait." He sat down to write, and begun thus: "You ask how I look, dearest mother? The hardships of this war have made me so old, that you would scarcely recognise me. On the right side of my head I am perfectly grey, my teeth are breaking and falling out, my face is as wrinkled as the frills of a lady's dress, my back as much bent as that of a monk of La Trappe; my heart alone remains unchanged, and so long as I live will preserve sentiments of the most affectionate esteem and faithful love for you, my dear, good mother." *

When the King read over this description of himself he broke out into a loud, merry laugh;

* Biography of a Patriotic Merchant.

then pushing the letter aside, he seized a pencil, and placed a sheet of paper before him.

There was profound silence in the royal apartment: outside was heard the monotonous pacing of the sentinels, and sometimes the sound of a trumpet, the neighing of a horse, or the word of command given by an officer.

The King heard nothing of all this; he was so accustomed to these sounds that they were entirely unheard and unheeded by him; and on this occasion he was so absorbed in his occupation, that he was not roused by the sudden and more than usually loud noise which interrupted the profound silence. He did not even hear a carriage roll into the courtyard of the palace, nor the vibrating gay notes of the post horn.

The Generals and staff, however, in the anteroom were instantly alive to these sounds. Nothing was more acceptable to them than any interruption of the monotony of these days of peace, for, accustomed to the excitement of war, and its heart-stirring events, they considered everything else tame, dull, and unendurable.

They therefore hurried to the windows, and looked with satisfaction at the muddy travelling calèche with its four panting, smoking post-horses standing at the portico. A tall, distinguished looking man got out of the carriage, and, disentangling himself from his furs, entered the palace.

The staff in the ante-room exchanged many suppositions as to who the new arrival could be, and they had just agreed that it was undoubtedly no other than the Marquis d'Argens, when the door opened and the stranger came in.

He asked for the aide-de-camp on service, and when he was pointed out he advanced towards him with a calm and dignified expression.

"I beg you will announce my arrival, without delay, to his Majesty. Be so good as to say that I have not come hither on my own affairs, but as ambassador from the city of Berlin, furnished with full powers by the magistracy and the burghers to request an audience of the King, and that I must return to Berlin as soon as possible."

"Your name, sir?"

"I am the merchant, Johann Gotzkowsky."

The grave and proud features of the courtly aide-de-camp immediately softened.

"Ah! Gotzkowsky, the rich and noble-hearted merchant of Berlin, the especial favourite of the King! I hasten to announce your arrival to his majesty."

And the aide-de-camp hurried through the room to the king's boudoir.

In the meantime the generals surrounded Gotzkowsky and heard from him all the details of the siege of Berlin, and the ruthless and cruel conduct of the enemy. They overwhelmed him with questions, and eagerly asked if he had met on his journey any of the enemy's troops, or heard of their being in the vicinity.

"You will find the King rather out of sorts, I fear," said General von Saldern. "He has not yet left his cabinet this morning, and, undoubtedly, he is occupied with very important affairs."

"With the plan of a battle, I suspect," said one of the other gentlemen; "for it is said Lacy has shoved his army forwards, and that

Landen has quitted Dresden. We shall probably thus have another battle, and the King is, no doubt, planning it at this moment."

The door of the adjoining room, where the King was, opened, and the aide-de-camp made a sign to Gotzkowsky to follow him. While he was traversing the ante-room, the generals strained their eyes to see into the King's cabinet, through the half-open door, anxious to examine the royal countenance, to judge from it whether this insufferable cessation of hostilities was likely to yield to the tumult of active strife.

In the meantime Gotzkowsky entered the royal cabinet, and the door was closed behind him. He was alone with the monarch, who was still seated at his writing table, drawing busily with his pencil on the paper before him.

"He is writing," said Gotzkowsky, mentally; "probably the plan of battle which his generals are awaiting with such eager impatience. It is strange to think that each stroke of his pen may, perhaps, cost the lives of hundreds of men." And he dared not, by a word, nor even by a breath, make his presence remarked.

The King, on his entrance, had merely casually cast on him one of those piercing and fiery glances, whose despotic power had caused many a general and many a hero to shrink, and had then quietly resumed his occupation.

Profound silence reigned for some time. The King suddenly interrupted it by making a sign to Gotzkowsky to come up to him.

"See if you like that!" said he, good-humouredly. "You are well known to be a judge of the fine arts, and have given me proofs that you understand painting. Look at this, and tell me if it pleases you."

So saying, he gave the paper with which he had been occupied to Gotzkowsky, with a friendly nod.

What was it that the King had drawn on the paper? Was it really, as his valiant generals desired, a plan for some dreadful battle? Was it a philosophical treatise; one of those witty and piquant epistles with which the

King favoured his friends? Not one of all these.

"A bouquet of flowers!" cried Gotzkowsky, looking first at the paper and then at the King, with undisguised astonishment.

"Your Majesty is sketching a bunch of flowers, while your generals in the next room confided to me that your Majesty was probably forming your plans for a battle, and that the Austrians are on the march."

"Nonsense," said the King, shrugging his shoulders. "My wild staff there invariably call out for war. They want nothing but fighting, and always to be hacking at their enemies. Don't pay any attention to them, but rather tell me if you like this drawing. Do you think that these roses interspersed with lilies will have a good effect? Ah! I see; you wish to know for what purpose it is destined? —for a service of porcelain which I am going to have painted here for the Marquis d'Argens;" and, meeting Gotzkowsky's eye, the King continued, with a smile, "Ah! you are rich—you can make what presents you choose; but the King of Prussia is a poor man—he has nothing but his sword, his uniform, and his china;* and that even," said the King, frowning, "I must procure from Meissen."

"You shall no longer require to do that, your Majesty," cried Gotzkowsky; "your own country shall now produce porcelain."

"Will you pledge yourself to this?" asked the King, evidently much pleased. "Will you undertake to manage it?"

"I will."

"If you say so, you are quite the man to carry it through," said the King. "I am extremely pleased with you, for you have fully justified the confidence I reposed in you when I was Crown Prince, and you have fulfilled your promise."

"I swore to your Majesty to be faithful to my country, and to serve it to the utmost extent of my means," cried Gotzkowsky, with noble ardour.

"And you have done so. It is by no means difficult to find people to serve the State in

* Biography of a Patriotic Merchant.

happy and fortunate times, but the really valuable citizens are those who unselfishly devote their time, their property, and themselves to their country in the time of war and misfortune."

He gave Gotzkowsky an open letter, which was on his writing-table, and said "Read that. It is a letter from the Marquis d'Argens. Read it aloud—I should like to hear it again."

Gotzkowsky read, with a faltering voice and with cheeks dyed by the blush of modesty, the following passages from the Marquis's letter, which the finger of the King pointed out :—

"Gotzkowsky is, indeed, an admirable man and a worthy citizen. I wish you had a number like him. The most valuable gift which fortune can bestow on a State is a burgher full of zeal for his King and his country; and in this respect I must say that, to the credit of Berlin, I saw many of its inhabitants in these critical times, with Gotzkowsky at their head, whose virtues would have been immortalised by the ancient Roman historians if they had lived in these days."

"Are you satisfied?" asked the King, when Gotzkowsky had finished and given him back the letter. "Ah! I see: you are a very modest man, and are blushing like a girl. But now, tell me what brings you here? what does the city of Berlin want from me?"

"Your Majesty," said Gotzkowsky gravely, "Berlin only demands her good rights."

"And who wishes to deprive her of them?"

"Your Majesty."

The King frowned darkly, and his eyes shot a fierce glance at the bold speaker. But Gotzkowsky coolly continued: "I repeat that your Majesty attacks our privileges, inasmuch as you wish to prevent our being honest men, and fulfilling our faithful promise."

"Oh! now I understand you," said the King, smiling. "You allude to the Russian war contribution—Berlin will not pay it."

"Excuse me, your Majesty, Berlin is resolved to pay it, that she may retain your gracious favour—she will pay it that the great Frederick may not have cause to blush for his faithless and dishonoured city, in that case unworthy to be called the royal capital and residence of our sovereign. Could your Majesty ever again place confidence in men who hesitated to redeem their pledged word, and who looked on their promises only as mouse-traps, from which they can slip out as soon as a favourable opportunity offers, when the cat is no longer watching them? Berlin *must* pay, that our sons may not have cause to blush for their fathers—that posterity may not accuse Berlin of having been the first to brand herself with dishonour. We have pledged our word, and we must redeem that pledge."

"You must do nothing of the kind. I will not have it so," cried the King, angrily. "I choose to exercise reprisals. Payment of the Bamberg and Würtzburg bonds has been refused."

"But your Majesty certainly considers this refusal most unfair and dishonourable," interrupted Gotzkowsky; "and because you wish to punish these faithless States you are doubly severe on your poor city of Berlin, by depriving it of the only possession misfortune and necessity have left,—an honourable name. Your Majesty cannot mean this in earnest."

"Are you so anxious to get rid of your money?" asked the King. "What is the amount of the sum you still owe?"

"A million and a half," your Majesty.

The King stepped back and stared at Gotzkowsky in surprise. "And the Berlin citizens really insist on paying this enormous sum?"

"Yes, sire, because their word is pledged."

The King shook his head, looked thoughtful, and said: "You appear to me to be rather a dangerous agitator. A few weeks ago, after the fatal battle of Kunersdorf, I sent a courier express to Berlin, counselling the magistrates to prevail on the rich merchants and citizens to withdraw with all their possessions from Berlin. My advice was not followed, and you are the very man who incited them to disobey my wishes. In your singular perverseness you had the audacity to cut your way through the enemy in the very country where they were encamped; and if my Lieutenant von Prettswitz had not discovered you in the wood, and brought you to the village where I was, the probability is that your obstinate head would soon have been looking down from the point of some Cossack's lance. And why did you run such risks? Simply to assure me, that the wealthy Berliners preferred staying at home to taking flight. Truly you are a strange diplomatist! You rush right into danger and difficulty, merely to prove to your King that his subjects no longer choose to obey him."

Frederick had said these words with assumed indignation, but a smile played round his lips, and his large blue eyes looked at Gotzkowsky with a pleased and kindly expression.

"They do not comply with your Majesty's commands on this occasion," said the merchant, "precisely because they wish to remain worthy of being your Majesty's citizens and subjects."

The King fixed his eyes on Gotzkowsky steadily, and said: "Now tell me how you contrived to make the Berlin people so obstinate and yet so lavish?"

Gotzkowsky smiled. "Your Majesty's subjects prise their honour higher than their life."

The King shook his head hastily. "No good telling me that. Say at once how you managed,—but the truth—the truth! How did you succeed in inspiring my people with such spirit?"

"The truth, then, your Majesty, is, that it was only the spirit of fear, for the sagacious magistrates were too thankful to receive your Majesty's commands to withhold payment of the bonds, and I strove in vain to remind them of their pledged word and endangered honour."

"I knew it. I was sure of it," said the King, laughing. "My good Berliners love their money dearly, like all other selfish human beings."

"Well, sire, when I saw that they were deaf to the voice of honour I sounded the voice of cautious wisdom in their ears. I painted to them the terrors sure to ensue, if the foe returned to take a violent revenge on the faithless city. I assured them that the Russians would sequestrate instantly all our effects in Dantzig, Courland, and Lithuania; and that the Russian Commander in Chief threatened to affix our names on the walls of every Exchange in Europe as bankrupts."

"You visited the Russian camp, then?"

"A fortnight ago, your Majesty. The mayor of Berlin begged me to undertake the journey, to conclude some business matters left unsettled by General Tottleben's speedy retreat."

"And are they now arranged?"

"I was obliged to sign an obligation to General Tottleben, pledging myself to return to the Russian camp in one month, to negotiate with him further in the name of the merchants."

"I have been informed that the Russian General refused to accept the bonds for the war contribution without your security. Is this also true?"

"Perfectly true, sire."

The King's eyes beamed with benevolence. "D'Argens is right," said he, kindly. "Titus Livius and Cornelius Nepos would have written your history."

A long pause ensued. Gotzkowsky was bold enough to break it.

"Your Majesty, I feel convinced, now advises our paying the contribution?"

"The contribution shall be paid," said Frederick, abruptly; but, when Gotzkowsky burst forth with eager words of gratitude, the King made him a sign to be silent. "I mean," continued he, imperiously, "that I will pay the money, if it must be so. Return, therefore, to the Russian camp, according to your promise. Endeavour to obtain a diminution of the sum, or at least more favourable terms as to the delay granted for payment; but, if it cannot be otherwise, I am prepared to pay this million and a half for my good Capital. But you must, in return, do me a service."

"Thankfully, your Majesty, be it what it may," cried the merchant, eagerly. "I am ready to make any sacrifice for your Majesty, were it even that of life itself."

The King smiled. "Not quite so bad as that; though I mean to call on you for what appears to most men more difficult and trying than death,—I mean silence and secrecy."

And, while placing his hand condescendingly on Gotzkowsky's shoulder, he continued, "You must reveal to no human being what I have just told you; and only at the last moment, when necessity requires it, take the magistrates into your confidence."

"How, sire!" cried Gotzkowsky, sorrowfully. "Do you mean to deprive your Berlin citizens of the happiness they would feel in expressing their boundless gratitude and love to your Majesty? Berlin is not to know how gracious and generous their Sovereign has been towards them!"

"I am not fond of the tinkling of words, nor of the glitter of laurel wreaths," said the King. "The very men who crown us with bay-leaves, would often prefer crushing our heads with a crown of iron or of thorns. You must advance the money for the contribution, and I will repay it. This is the whole matter;—not a word more."* And in a hurried tone, as if

* The King in effect paid the contribution secretly, no one knew how, when, or where.—History of Frederick the Great, vol. ii. p. 256.

fearing that the merchant might still venture to oppose his wishes, he continued, "Now tell me something of Berlin, and, above all, of our Gallery at Sans Souci. What of it?"

"It is completed, your Majesty, and people throng thither in crowds."

"I alone must wander about like a fugitive or a Don Quixote," said the King, sadly, "unable even to cross the threshold of my own palace. This is what they call 'the happiness of being a king!'" said he in a low voice; and, turning to Gotzkowsky, he continued, "Have you seen the Gallery since the enemy left it?"

"Yes, your Majesty; Prince Esterhazy was the noble foe who guarded Sans Souci like a sacred shrine; and, when he quitted it, he only carried off one small picture as a remembrance." *

The King nodded. "I know it, and it is the only pleasure I have had for a long time. I shall one day again see the noble Titians and Correggios, the Rubens and Van Eycks, you

* Biography of a Patriotic Merchant.

purchased for me. But tell me now of Charlottenburg. What of it? but, above all, the truth! You dread my wrath? I see perfectly well that no one will speak plainly on the subject,—it is a point always evaded. You are a brave man, and do not even fear the Cossacks, —you will therefore have courage to speak the truth to your sovereign. What of Charlottenburg? I am resolved to know the worst. The Saxons took possession of it;—what did they do?"

Gotzkowsky, frequently interrupted by the King's exclamations of anger and indignation, related at full length the barbarous and ruthless vandalism exercised by the Saxons in the castle of Charlottenburg. He also detailed their shameless cruelties and love of destruction.

"And the Polignac Collection?" asked the King eagerly.

"It is almost totally destroyed."

The King started up from his arm chair, and his eyes shot fire. He was now no longer the philosopher of Sans Souci, no longer the poet, but the stern hero, breathing war and revenge: "Tell me all; I am determined to know every particular," said the King in fiery wrath.

When, however, Gotzkowsky detailed to him more fully the savage manner in which human beings had been tortured by these barbarians, and the sacred treasures of art ruthlessly devastated, the King's face darkened more perceptibly every minute, and his pale cheeks became flushed with rage. Once he raised his clasped hands to Heaven as if invoking lightning from above to blight those cruel savages. When Gotzkowsky had ended, the King said abruptly, "Enough, enough!" and, with hasty and agitated steps, he advanced to the door leading to the ante-room, and knocked loudly, calling "Saldern," in a loud voice. General von Saldern immediately appeared. The King commanded him to close the door and to come forward, and said, in an abrupt and resolute tone, "You are to go to-morrow, with a strong detachment of cavalry and infantry, to Hubertsburg. Take possession of the castle, make a list of all valuables in it, and have them carefully packed, and afterwards sold. I will appropriate none of it. I mean to assign the money they fetch to the Lazaretto, and not forget you either." A pause ensued. General von Saldern stood motionless near the door, in a stiff military attitude. The King looked at him in surprise, "Well, did you hear what I said?"

"I heard your Majesty," said the general; "but, sire, you must pardon me for saying that such a command is contrary to my honour and my oath."

The King evidently strove to be calm, for he prized General Saldern as a noble minded and valuable officer.

"You might possibly be right," said he, "if I did not intend to use this desperate means for a good purpose. The heads of the great and noble of the earth do not suffer when the hair of their subjects is torn out; those must be attacked where they are susceptible. I do so now. The Elector of Saxony shall feel what it is to have one's most precious possessions destroyed. We will teach him a lesson of civilization and humanity. Go therefore forthwith to Hubertsburg, as I commanded you."

General Saldern's face turned pale, and deep emotion was depicted in his countenance as he gravely but firmly answered, "Were your Majesty to order me instantly to go to meet the enemy and to seize their batteries, or to lead a forlorn hope, I would cordially obey, but I neither dare nor can act contrary to the voice of duty, honour, and my oath."

The King stamped furiously on the floor, and shaking his clenched fist at the general, he said, in a tone of thunder, "You will obey me instantly, according to your bounden duty; the only voice you have to listen to is that of your sovereign and master."

General Saldern calmly replied, "Pardon me, your Majesty, I must again repeat that the voice of honour must be paramount. Your Majesty can easily transfer this order to another."

The King turned away, frowning darkly; he went up to Saldern, and laying his hand on his shoulder, said in a softened voice, "Hear me,

Saldern; you have but to obey, the responsibility rests with me. Go to Hubertsburg."

"I cannot, your Majesty."

"You do not care then to enrich yourself? so far well!" said the King; "but you are dismissed my service. I cannot employ a soldier who does not consider obedience his primary duty."

"I must then resign my command into your Majesty's hand?"

"Undoubtedly! Do so, and leave me instantly."*

General von Saldern made a silent and profound military obeisance, and left the room.

"You also," said the King to Gotzkowsky, who had been an involuntary and silent witness of this painful scene, "go, and desire my aide-de-camp to send me immediately Quintus Icilius."

* This conversation of the King with General von Saldern is historical, and literally true, word for word. General von Saldern quitted the army, but was restored after the peace with high honours and distinctions.—Traits of General von Saldern, by Küster, Berlin, 1793, page 39.

A few minutes afterwards, Major Quintus Icilius entered the room.

"Repair to Hubertsburg with a detachment of cavalry and infantry, and clear out the palace," said the King, harshly.

Icilius carefully avoided opposing the royal will. He had already heard in the adjoining apartment of Saldern's fate; moreover, this commission was by no means contrary to his own inclinations.

"You must pay over 100,000 dollars to the Lazaretto, the rest you can retain for yourself," said the King.

"I obey your Majesty. Shall we set off to-day?"

The King looked at him with a frown. "Are you in such a hurry to enrich yourself by plunder?" said he. "Leave the room. I will appoint the time and hour presently."*

* In May, 1761, the command of the King was put into execution. Major Quintus Icilius devastated and plundered the Castle of Hubertsburg in a most barbarous manner, leaving nothing but the bare broken walls. The King was apparently pleased, but when the major, in

When the King was once more alone he paced his cabinet, absorbed in thought. For a time he remained standing at the window, and casting up his bright blue eyes to heaven, with a sorrowful expression, he said, sighing, "Poor fools that we are! We have but a passing moment to live, and yet we embitter this moment as much as we can, and rejoice in destroying the masterpieces of industry and art; thus erecting a never dying monument of our own shame and barbarism."*

the year 1764, demanded compensation for his captains, for the money they had expended in recruiting, the King wrote with his own hand on the margin of the petition, "His officers stole like ravens; they shall get nothing."

* The King's own words.

## WINTER QUARTERS IN LEIPZIG.

The King of Prussia had left Meissen and taken up his winter quarters in Leipzig. The choice of this city had been caused by a peculiar circumstance. The King wished to pass the winter in a town with a university, in order to substitute the society of philosophers and artists, poets and sculptors, for the privations and dangers of war. He sent for his royal band of musicians from Berlin, and invited the professors of the Leipzig University to his table.

Thus was Leipzig—that rich and luxurious mercantile city—transformed for a few months into a royal residence. But the change had been very reluctantly submitted to by the inhabitants; and it was quite contrary to the wishes of the community that they were obliged to receive the Prussian King within their walls instead of the allied troops. The King was well aware of this, and showed no wish to spare the wealth and resources of the town whose unwelcome guest he was.

If Leipzig had received the Prussian army more readily, such exactions on her means would not have been made; but the insolent and sulky demeanour of the inhabitants towards the King of Prussia, their warm enthusiasm for Austria, the ally of Saxony, naturally embittered Frederick and increased his extortions. As Leipzig chose to consider the Prussians as enemies, the Prussians were equally forced to consider the Leipzigers as foes, and to treat them accordingly.

Enormous contributions were levied on the city; and, in spite of the previous written promise of the King that the levies on Leipzig should not exceed 500,000 dollars, new calls were constantly made. In vain did the magistrates implore and entreat for mercy and justice; in vain did the merchants protest that their means were exhausted, and that it was wholly out of their power to make any further payments. The demands were persisted in with an iron will, and, as the resisting city also persevered in its opposition, the most violent threats were resorted to, to terrify the inhabitants into compliance. Torches of pitch were hung from the roofs of the houses, and the burning of the whole town, which they swore to reduce to ashes, was threatened by the Prussians if the Leipzigers did not forthwith pay the million of dollars exacted. But the unhappy inhabitants had reached that extremity of despair, when there is no longer either fear or anxiety, for there is nothing more to lose. They declared that they could not pay, and offered to substantiate their words by death.

The inflammable pitch torches were, indeed, removed from the houses, but the richest and most highly respected citizens were seized and imprisoned; the civic dignitaries themselves were not spared; and some of the highest magistrates were thrown into the city prison. They inclosed them like a flock of sheep, in the most degrading manner, in rooms which scarcely could contain such numbers of victims. Wet straw formed their couches; their only food was bread and water, brought to them by their Prussian gaolers, who loaded them with abuse and opprobrium.

Even these very turnkeys felt the burden too heavy for them; they tired of their odious office, and tried to escape from it. At first there were a hundred and twenty prisoners, but, after fourteen days of intolerable cruelty and insults, they set free the greater number, only retaining seventeen, who, indeed, were the richest and most distinguished men in Leipzig. These poor hostages, all spoiled sons of wealth and luxury, were now forced to bear the whole burden of misfortune, and the fury of the victorious foe. They whose mode of living had made them delicate and fastidious were now forced to submit to the greatest privations and the most painful sufferings The cold ground was their bed; a morsel of bread cast to them their food; and it was a day of rejoicing for them when one of the fair ladies of Leipzig succeeded in gaining access to an imprisoned husband or brother, smuggling in, under cover of their wide silk cloaks, a bit of meat or a jar of soup to these unfortunate captives.*

These cruelties would, undoubtedly, have been not only lessened, but entirely abrogated, if the King had been made aware of their existence, or if he had really believed that the declared inability of Leipzig to pay its subsidy was, in fact, no pretence, but the actual truth; but the King, weary of never ending complaints, and displeased by the perverse conduct of Leipzig, remembering, likewise, the odious vandalism of the Saxons in Charlottenburg, had issued the strictest orders not to plague him further on this subject, until he could be told that the imposed contribution was paid.

This sealed the doom of the unfortunate inhabitants of Leipzig. No one now dared to represent to the King the tortures and cruelties to which the hostages of the unhappy city were exposed. No one had courage to interfere in their favour, whose only crime con-

* Von Archenholz: Seven Years' War, page, 211.

sisted in their wealth being exhausted, and, consequently, being unable to pay the enormous sums demanded.

Whilst, however, this severe time of trial and suffering assailed the population of the town, perfect tranquillity and peace reigned in the house which the King of Prussia occupied. There was music and reading; and, amongst these pleasant recreations and agreeable stillness, Frederick sketched the plan for his next campaign, and for new and great exploits.

He had sent for Fasch and Quanz from Berlin to conduct the music, for the Marquis d'Argens to talk philosophy with him, and for his little dogs to play with.

The King, who had sufficient knowledge of men to despise from his heart these poor feeble, irresolute, and erring beings, had, however, a sufficient knowledge of dogs, to induce him to love with his whole heart those faithful, obedient, and loving creatures, and he bestowed no little love and care on them. He who turned a deaf ear to the sorrows and lamentations of a whole city was keenly alive to the smallest complaint of his "Biche," or "Psyche," and he never would have forgiven any one who had ventured to treat one of his dogs, as they did many noble and worthy men of Leipzig in his name.

## A FRIEND IN NEED.

Time passed on, and yet no one ventured to disobey the King's command, by appealing to him on behalf of the persecuted prisoners; even the Marquis d'Argens, the intimate friend and confidant of Frederick, had declined to intercede for the inhabitants of the city. They appeared irretrievably lost, and a still worse doom threatened them. The heads of the first houses and families, now languishing in gloomy dungeons, had been told that it was intended to transport them to Magdeburg as recruits, and to send them thither on foot, with their knapsacks on their backs—but in the hour of need a deliverer was to appear in this extremity. A tall proud figure was seen crossing the antechamber of the King: strength and energy were depicted on his features, and his eyes beamed with a noble enthusiasm. The task from which courtiers and flatterers shrank he is about to undertake; and what even the bravest generals do not dare he will dare. Johann Gotzkowsky is resolved to make the King hear truth—he does not hesitate to rouse the royal wrath when the object is to aid the unhappy, to succour the persecuted. He has a nobler mission to fulfil than to strive to win the smile of a king, or tokens of favour from the great—it is the mission of humanity which impels him to the King's presence; and his resolve, as usual, stands firm and immutable.

With undaunted courage he places his hand on the lock of the door leading to the royal apartment. He could enter unannounced, for the King expected him. He had summoned Gotzkowsky from Berlin, to learn from him details of the progress of the Berlin Industrial Institution. The noble patriot had therefore in obedience to the King's command arrived in Leipzig; he had seen the misery and wretchedness of this crushed and persecuted city; and while he was crossing the ante-room he had inwardly thought, with a smile, "I won over the

Russian general to mildness and forbearance, surely I shall not find the King more obdurate than he was."

But, before casting aside his cloak, he took from it a small packet, which he carefully examined, and, apparently satisfied by the result, he took it with him, and entered the royal cabinet.

At first Frederick took no notice of him. He was lying on the floor, surrounded by his little dogs on silk cushions, their bright eyes eagerly fixed on a dish placed in the middle, from which the King was at this moment, with careful impartiality, and with the aid of an ivory spoon, apportioning to each of his dogs their share of the meal; while, enjoining quiet and patience on those who were growling and eagerly snapping, he fed with his own hands those who were waiting decorously for their turn to come.

"Ah! you are laughing," said Frederick, "and in your foolish blindness you think it quite beneath my dignity to occupy myself with dogs, when the society of men can be procured. I may just tell you you know nothing of the matter; you know nothing of dogs, and, probably little more of men. Be quiet, Biche; let Apollo's dinner alone—I gave it to him myself, and it is his own. I declare it looks as if you dogs had taken a lesson from men, and in the fulness of your Christian benevolence and love, were resolved to take the bread out of each other's mouths.—Be quiet, Biche! don't growl so loud; don't be angry that I compared you to a human being!—No wonder you are affronted."

The King fondly stroked and caressed the offended puppy, and then rising from the carpet he threw himself into an arm chair.

His piercing eye was fixed on Gotzskowsky, and quickly perceived the small packet which he held in his hand.

"What have you there?"

"A plate and a cup," said Gotzskowsky; "the first fruits of my porcelain manufactory in Berlin."

The King started from his chair, and went up hastily to Gotzskowsky.

"Give it to me," said he; "I want to see what kind of pottery you are pleased to call china."

The King impatiently snatched off the paper covering, and was so eager about it that he did not observe that Apollo and Biche were already by the ears about a scrap of paper which the King had thrown down, and which they, thinking it some delicate morsel, had considered well worth contending for.

"Upon my word this is beautiful china!" cried the King, withdrawing the gilt-edged plate and the beautifully painted cup from the paper, and closely examining them. As his eye rested on the painting of the cup, his features assumed a sad and softened expression.

"My house at Rheinsberg!" murmured he in a low voice; "a greeting from my happiest days!"

"I had the honour of being first presented to your Majesty in the palace of Rheinsberg," said Gotzkowsky; "it is therefore especially precious in my sight, and I resolved it should adorn the first specimen produced by my porcelain manufactory."

The King cast a searching glance at him: "You are telling me a fairy tale—I am no friend of such legends. Say the truth, therefore,—where did you get this porcelain? I see it is not from Meissen, for the crossed swords, the well-known mark, is wanting; besides it is stronger and whiter—where did you get it?"

"In Berlin, sire. I said to your Majesty in Meissen that you should one day find your own country furnish your porcelain, and I was forced to do all honour to my promise."

"You have created a porcelain fabric by your breath."

"By the breath of gold, your Majesty."

"Tell me all about it, every detail," said the King, still holding the cup in his hand, and looking at it attentively.

Gotzkowsky related to him that, immediately after his return from Meissen, he had by chance made the acquaintance of a young man who was passing through Berlin on his way to

Gotha, the duke there having promised to advance him capital to found a manufactory, in which porcelain was to be prepared according to his directions.* The specimens he showed Gotzkowsky convinced him that this stranger was thoroughly acquainted with the mysteries of porcelain fabrication; he had therefore instantly formed the resolution to tempt away this artist from Gotha. Money had here, as everywhere, its usual magic power, and all that was necessary was to offer more favourable terms than those proposed by the Duke of Gotha in his contract. For some thousand more dollars, and double purchase money, Gotzkowsky had bought the secret of making the finest china, and also induced the manufacturer to settle in Berlin.† He had made

* Von Archenholz.

† The manufacture of china was at that time a great mystery, only known in Germany, at Meissen. The mixture of clay for china was made with locked doors, and by workmen who were bound by oath to the strictest secrecy. Herr Wegely had already, before Gotzkowsky,

the necessary arrangements for the first trials in some buildings behind his house; and the pieces he had brought the King were the first fruits of his manufactory.

The King listened to him with eager attention, and when he finished nodded and smiled.

"The Marquis d'Argens is right," said he; "I wish I had many citizens like you. It would be a fine thing to be a King if those we ruled over were all true men, worth the trouble of being to them a kind father and master. You have fulfilled one of my most cherished wishes; and I must say that I do not imagine you will long call this porcelain manufactory your own; I think it will soon become a royal establishment.*"

"I founded it on purpose for your Majesty.'

established a manufactory of china, but, owing to its inferiority, it soon was given up.

* Gotzkowsky paid for this secret 10,000 dollars in cash, and a yearly income for life to the discoverer, of 1,000 dollars, besides firewood and lodging.—Biography of a Patriotic Merchant, p. 87.

"Good, good! you have caused me real pleasure; I will endeavour to do the same to you. Ask a favour—you hesitate! Have you nothing to ask for?"

"I have indeed, your Majesty," said Gotzkowsky eagerly; "I have a very great favour to ask—Have pity on the poor inhabitants of this city."

The King frowned sternly, and compressed his lips suddenly.

"Do you know that I have strictly prohibited any one molesting me with the complaints of these Leipzigers?"

"I do know it, your Majesty."

The King looked at him in surprise.

"And yet you have done so?"

"I ventured to do so, your Majesty, because I relied on the great and magnanimous heart of my sovereign; and common humanity compelled me not to fear even your Majesty's anger, when the object was to succour the oppressed."

"So you wished to bribe me beforehand with your trumpery china? You are a good calculator, but this time you shall find you are far wrong in your calculations. These perverse, obstinate Leipzigers shall have no pity from me; they must pay the 100,000 dollars or—"

"Or?" asked Gotzkowsky, eagerly, as the King hesitated.

Frederick looked at him angrily. "You are very bold," said he, "to interrupt me. They must pay because I require the money for my troops, and the Leipzigers are rich; they are well able to pay."

"They are quite unable, your Majesty. They can meet your demand as little as Berlin can meet that of Russia, unless their generous King assists them. I am sure your Majesty cannot wish that it should be recorded in the pages of history, that Russia acted with more mildness and generosity towards Berlin, than Prussia did towards Leipzig. It is true that the Russians have thrown into prison some of the oldest Jews because they did not pay; but at least they treated these poor victims of their rapacity like men; they did not make them sleep on foul straw, or starve in filth and misery; they neither scourged nor tortured them till blood mingled with their tears."

"Who dares to do that?" cried the King in a voice of thunder.

Gotzkowsky made a deep obeisance, and said in a low but distinct voice—

"His Majesty the King of Prussia."

The King started up, and raised his arm against Gotzkowsky with a gesture of fierce rage; but the merchant fixed his calm steady eye on him without flinching.

"It is a lie!" called out the King; "recal it instantly!"

"Through the course of a long life I have always spoken the truth, your Majesty—the truth, without dread or fear of mortal man. Your Majesty is the first person who has ever accused me of falsehood. I have seen, with my own eyes, your Majesty's officials treat the poor imprisoned men of Leipzig like dogs—but what do I say—like dogs? Ah! how thankful would these poor starving persecuted men be—how they would envy your dogs the dish before them, which contains what would be a feast to the prisoners! It may be right, your Majesty, to imprison and humiliate the refractory, but not to crush out the very soul of a man. Even in the vanquished, God's image should be honoured, and not insulted and defaced."

The King looked at him in surprise, and yet apparently not displeased.

"Are you going to give me a lecture?" said he, after a pause. "Well, I forgive you for this once. I honour in you, as you say, God's image, and also respect the possessor of the porcelain manufactory—but no more of these unruly Leipzigers. They must pay. My soldiers cannot live upon air, and my treasury is at last fairly exhausted."

"The Leipzigers are quite ready to pay according to their ability; but the demand must not exceed their means."

"How do you know this?"

"The magistrates and merchants of Leipzig sent me a deputation to entreat my mediation in their behalf."

"You are then it appears well known as a

man who can make good use of his tongue, and turn it to account."

"Your Majesty," said Gotzkowsky smiling, "we follow the example of our hero King; we are ready to fight with any one, and those who have no sword must fight with their tongues. The Leipzig people had probably heard that I have had considerable practice in this way recently, and that I won a victory over the Russians which had good results."

"How much do you think this city is prepared to offer?" asked the King.

"If your Majesty will remit 300,000 dollars, and give the merchants time, they will give you solid bonds and bills, which they bind themselves to discharge."

"Parbleu! a fine idea!" cried the King with a sneer. "The bills and bonds of Leipzig merchants are no security at all: but," added Frederick with a smile suddenly, "will you become their guarantee?"

"If your Majesty desires it, the bills shall be accepted by me."

"I am then to look to you, and consider you as their security for payment?"

"Undoubtedly, your Majesty."

"In that case, for your sake, I will exempt the Leipzigers from the payment of 300,000 dollars; but you become responsible for the liquidation of the other 800,000."

"I pledge myself for that sum, your Majesty."

"I shall take care that these Leipzig gentlemen know that it is to your intercession they owe this diminution of the contribution demanded. Moreover, you have my full permission to exact a handsome recompense from this wealthy city for the service you have rendered them if you choose."

"I don't choose, by any means, sire," said Gotzkowsky, in noble indignation. "I grieve that your Majesty should think so meanly of me as to imagine that I would accept a profit from the misfortunes of others, and that I only supplicate you in favour of these poor people to derive pecuniary benefit for myself."*

"I'll tell you what I think of you—that you are a self-willed, obstinate, hard-headed man,

* Biography of a Patriotic Merchant.

who must take his own way, and do as he pleases," said the King with an amused smile; "but I am ready to admit, however, that you have in your own way done me much good service. I shall, therefore, always be kindly disposed towards you; and you have left some very valuable memorials of yourself in my gallery at Sans Souci."

"When your Majesty returns thither you will also find the Correggio there, about which your Majesty wrote to the Marquis d'Argens."

The King's eyes brightened. "That Correggio is mine!" said he, while slowly pacing the room, with his hands behind his back.

"Ah!" said he at length in a low voice, as if to himself, "when will this weary pilgrimage be over, and the pacified world grant to the poor King some leisure and refreshment—some happy hours to enjoy his home and his pictures? The Wandering Jew, if he ever existed, has not led a life of more constant change than I have done. I have become at last like those strolling players who have neither hearth nor home. Like them, we wander through the world, producing dismal tragedies, and employ ing the lamentations of our subjects as our chorus. When is this to end?"*

"When your Majesty has vanquished all your foes," cried Gotzkowsky.

The King looked round in surprise; he had quite forgotten his presence.

"Ah! you are still here?" asked he. "So you prophesy victory for me? Before you go home, impress on the Leipzigers that they must make haste with their payments. When you visit Potsdam greet my Correggio from me, and say that I long to see him, as ardently as a lover does his bride. Adieu!"

* The King's own words. *Vide* Correspondance de Frederic II. avec le Comte Algarotti.

## REWARDS AND THANKS.

GOTZKOWSKY had thus freed unhappy Leipzig from the heavy burden which had crushed it to the earth. The prisoners were released, and the merchants granted bonds to the amount of 800,000 dollars, for the just and prompt payment of which Gotzkowsky pledged himself, and affixed his signature to the papers. He did not do so from any selfish motive, nor from a vainglorious thirst for fame; not to exalt his name in the eyes of the world, nor to increase his collection of public testimonials of gratitude; but from the pure love of mankind; because he wished strictly to fulfil the vow he had made to God when a trembling starving boy on the public highway—that, if ever he became rich, he would be to the needy and oppressed the same succouring hand which had been extended to him in the cloud of dust, and which rescued him from despair. He did so, as he says with much *naïveté* and simplicity in the "History of his Life," "because I knew from my own experience how severe it is on a city to collect such an enormous sum; and it would have been most repulsive to my feelings to have profited by the miseries of the times."

Again a brilliant banquet was given in honour of Gotzkowsky; words of gratitude were spoken, tears of emotion shed, and lofty promises innumerable uttered. This commemoration was given by the merchants of Leipzig to him who had so nobly pleaded their cause, and got them exempted from 300,000 dollars, countersigning their bonds. They consumed the most costly food in his honour, drank the rarest wines to his health, and did homage to him in the most solemn orations.

When Gotzkowsky, weary and exhausted by this feast, returned to his quarters, he found three letters on his table. One, which bore the Prussian arms on its seal, he opened first. It was a private order from the King of Prussia on his confidential secretary Leinning to pay

100,000 dollars to Johann Gotzkowsky, merchant.*

"So much to account!" said Gotzkowsky smiling. "I have purchased pictures for the King to the amount of 100,000 ducats, and the King, it appears, does not intend to remain my debtor for ever." With a slight shrug, Gotzkowsky broke open the second letter. Suddenly he laughed loudly, and his features assumed an amused and sneering expression.

"The Elector of Saxony, in consideration of my services to the city of Leipzig, appoints me his Privy Councillor of Commerce," cried he laughing, and waving the paper in the air. "Ah! this is really a capital joke. The petty Elector, who has been in my debt for many long years, confers a mark of distinction on me, and throws me a crumb of dignity—a title! Many thanks! My own name sounds quite good enough for me. I need no titles to be an honest man; they may please a vain fool, but not me."†

* Biography of a Patriotic Merchant.

† Goztkowsky never would assume this title. *Vide* his Life, page 143.

So saying, he cast aside the paper contemptuously, and took up the third letter; but, when he read it, proud joy lighted up his noble features, and his eyes beamed with pleasure.

This third letter was an address of thanks from the magistrates of Leipzig, gratefully acknowledging his disinterested and benevolent mediation in their favour, and declaring the merchants and the entire community his debtors for ever.

"I will present this paper to my daughter to preserve as a memorial of the gratitude and good will of the people of Leipzig," said Gotzkowsky; and, while folding it up again, he added thoughtfully, "Who knows if a time may not come, when Elise may be forced to remind the merchants of Berlin, of the promises contained in this address? The ideas and intentions of men are very uncertain and changeable."

But Gotzkowsky himself was destined to remind ungrateful Leipzig of its proffered gratitude, not to claim the bestowal of any services in return, but simply to protect himself from calumny, and base insinuations against his honour. For a day did actually come when Leipzig had forgotten its extremity and need, and only remembered Johann Gotzkowsky as a creditor to whom they owed enormous sums. When at length, tired of vainly waiting, he pressed them for payment, they accused him of selfish covetousness, and declared that his interference in their affairs had been quite unnecessary, and that it would have been far better if he had not succeeded in getting them out of prison at that time. There would have been, certainly, a good deal to suffer, but less money to sacrifice.

Gotzkowsky met these accusations in the way most analogous to his proud and noble nature—he was silent. But now new times of suffering and persecution were inflicted on the rich city of Leipzig. The Prussian King demanded fresh contributions, and then the inhabitants remembered the good service Gotzkowsky had once done them, and sent him humble letters, imploring him to have compassion on their need. The shrewd magistrates thought it politic to take notice of the previous calumnies against Gotzkowsky, which they had, a short time before, purposely disseminated in all the public papers, and solemnly declared, through the same medium, "Truth demands from us the acknowledgment of all the kindness and benevolence which Johann Gotzkowsky showed to this city, both in past years and at the last Leipzig fair, for which we have the strongest reasons to be deeply grateful.*

Gotzkowsky overlooked the offence, and once more assisted them, by persuading the King of Prussia to reduce the sum demanded; and he again guaranteed the payment of the bills granted by the merchants.

Once more the magistrates and merchants thanked him, in the most touching and moving words, for his noble and unselfish intercession; and yet they were one day a second time to prove how entirely they had forgotten all gratitude.

* Gotzkowsky's Life, page 160.

## FOUR YEARS LATER.

Four years of labour, industry, and stirring activity had passed away since the stormy year 1760. They had brought little change in the life of Gotzkowsky and his daughter.

Gotzkowsky toiled and worked on as he had always done. His manufactories were enlarged, his riches augmented, and his mercantile fame resounded through the whole world.

But he would have gladly sacrificed all those advantages, could he have seen one gay smile on the lips of his child, or restored to her the bloom and cheerfulness of former days.

The once lovely and impassioned girl was transformed into a grave, pale, silent woman, who had learned how to throw a veil of quiet resignation over the secret sorrows of her heart, and to suppress all outward signs of the sufferings which still saddened her whole being.

Elise had grown old within herself—old, in spite of her twenty-two years. She contemplated life as an arid, dreary desert, which she was doomed to wander through, with bleeding feet and bruised heart. In her feeling of utter desolation she shrunk from her own existence. No sound, no syllable, no outward sign of woe was ever to relieve the deathlike monotony of her life.

She had neither wishes nor hopes. Her grief was exhausted. She wept no more—she strove no longer with her love, for she had renounced it; but she could not bring herself to take an interest in fresh joys, she could only be resigned.

She had accepted life, and she endured it as the captive bird does, who, wounded and imprisoned in a gilded cage, is deprived of freedom and the pure air of heaven, and thus doomed to a prolonged existence of splendid misery.

She too was a poor captive bird, whose wounded heart and shattered frame, with broken and weary wing, pined away in mournful sadness and exhaustion within her father's luxurious mansion.

In the midst of the pomp and splendour which surrounded the admired daughter of the rich man, she felt herself solitary, forsaken, and utterly miserable.

She prayed to God for peace,—no longer for happiness. She had sunk into a state of apathy which asks nothing more than a still and dreamy existence, equally devoid of pleasure or of pain. Her sorrows were not softened by the religious feeling that they were all sent by a Higher Power.

The misfortunes which God thinks fit to send, bear within them the spiritual power of consolation; and, though we may be hurled to the earth, humbled and cast down, still a healing power is vouchsafed to us—strength is bestowed, to suffer with patience and resignation.

But it is otherwise with the misfortunes which proceed from men, which their wicked schemes, malice, or malignity, cause us to suffer; we have neither comfort nor refreshment; we are a prey to bitterness and woe; we are humiliated and oppressed, and even our burning tears cannot wash away our misery, or again invigorate and purify our hearts.

If her lover had been snatched from her by the hand of death, had she lost him by giving him up to God, Elise would have submitted to this sad but holy sorrow, and even considered it as a blessing in disguise intended to purify her heart, and the hope of a blissful reunion in eternity would have been a sovereign balm to her sorrow.

But she had lost him by his own treachery; she had resigned him to another, the victim of his desertion and faithlessness; she had renounced him for ever, not for a short space of time, but to all eternity; and she dared not even weep for him, for her misfortune was also her disgrace, and her very tears caused her humiliation and shame.

She had never spoken either to her father or to Bertram of the painful and dreary past, of the errors and delusions of her young days, and neither had ventured, in their faithful and considerate love, to intrude on the silence under which Elise had buried her grief.

She was now an humble attentive daughter to her father, and to Bertram a confiding and affectionate sister; but both felt that her poor broken heart only gave them the fragments of love and trust, which had been saved from the shipwreck of her happiness. Both knew that Elise had no full and entire heart to offer them, but only an empty and broken one. They were thankful, however, even for these shattered fragments of the once fair temple, and happy to be able to collect even the scattered leaves of the rose cut down by the storm, and to recal how beautiful it once was in its bloom.

Gotzkowsky's sole desire was that his daughter should live and regain her health, and acquire strength to re-create fresh happiness in her young life.

Bertram, in the strength and truth of his feelings towards her, had no other wish than one day to see her again cheerful and happy,— her b eing once more lighted up by that sunshine which love and felicity alone can ever shed on the human face. And in his strong and self-sacrificing attachment, he said to himself, "If I only knew that her happiness and peace of mind lay in the furthest corner of the world, I would gladly go thither to obtain it for her, even were I thus to lose her for ever."

Thus four years passed, outwardly all sunshine and brightness in the eyes of the world, brilliantly diversified by riches and splendour; inwardly, dull and desolate, full of privation and suppressed sorrow.

---

## THE DAY OF MISFORTUNE.

GOTZKOWSKY was alone in his room; it was an elegant, beautifully decorated apartment, which the greatest prince might well have envied.

The most rare pictures of celebrated ancient masters hung on the walls; the most precious porcelain vases stood on gilt brackets between the paintings; there were costly Italian marble pillars; the space between the windows was filled by splendid Venetian mirrors, and beautifully executed Grecian marble statues adorned the room.

The furniture was simple, for Gotzkowsky had only one passion, to gratify which he every year spent enormous sums; this was his collections of *vertù*—his bronzes, marbles, pictures, and antique gems. His house resembled a temple of art, for it contained the most prized treasures; and when Gotzkowsky, with his daughter, entered this room and gazed at his pictures along with her, or contemplated with delight his exquisite statues, his eye beamed with satisfaction, and his whole being was inspired with cheerfulness.

On this day, however, he wore a sad and anxious expression, and, though his pictures looked down on him from the walls above, with the same sublime and kindly glances he knew so well, yet his eye remained dim and troubled, and deep anxiety was depicted on his countenance.

He was seated at his writing table searching among papers, huge piles of which were heaped up before him. Sometimes his face assumed an expression of alarm and uneasiness, and his whole frame trembled, while, with a hurried hand, he made notes from some of the papers; suddenly he dropped his pen, and pressed his hand to his forehead, "It is in vain!" whispered he, "in vain! even were I to collect my whole strength, and risk all I have in the world on this one call, it would not suffice to pay these enormous sums."

Again he examined the papers, and, pointing

to one in particular, he continued, "Yes, there it stands; I am a wealthy man on paper; Leipzig owes me more than a million. If that payment were made, and De Neufville arrives, I am saved—but if this be not so? If Leipzig on this occasion, as it has done three times previously, pretends inability to pay,—if De Neufville should fail to come,—what am I to do in that case? How shall I then save myself from shame and dishonour?" He gazed in dreamy sadness at the papers before him; a dreadful feeling of intolerable anguish oppressed his vital powers, and drove all the blood from his heart to his head. He started from his chair, muttering some broken words expressive of the misery and horror of his soul. He remained standing, pressing both his hands to his head, as if wishing to subdue the torturing pain which made all his pulses beat, and his head feel like lead. "Oh, this is dreadful!" said he, in a faltering voice. "I stand on the brink of a precipice with my eyes open: I see it plainly; and yet I cannot avoid it. If no helping hand is stretched out to me I must be precipitated, and my good name destroyed along with me! and to think that it is neither rashness, speculation, nor folly which have brought me to these straits, but my love for mankind—for my fellow creatures! I never failed to extend a saving hand to any of my brethren who implored my aid; I never refused my assistance to those who required it—and solely for this, for the good I have done, I now stand on the brink of this frightful abyss."

He raised his eyes to heaven dimmed with tears. "Was it wrong, Heavenly Father," said he, sadly, "was it deserving of punishment, that I trusted my fellow creatures, and am I doomed to lose my honour for having acted with love and charity?"

But this state of misery and dejection did not last long. Gotzkowsky roused himself from his grief, and, proudly raising his head as if to shake off the load of care which crushed him to the earth, he said in a resolute tone, "I must not lose courage: this eventful day demands all my self-possession and presence of mind, and the decisive moment shall neither find me timid nor faint hearted."

He was about to resume his labours, when a repeated knocking at the door disturbed him. He reluctantly called to the person to come in, and Bertram entered.

"I beg your pardon," said he, shyly; "I know that you wish to be alone, but I could no longer bear it; I felt that I must see you. Remember, that I only returned here a fortnight ago, and I have scarcely seen you since; do not, therefore, be angry with me for having acted contrary to your orders in coming here, though I knew that you were much occupied."

Gotzkowsky nodded to him with a sad smile. "Thank you for coming," said he; "I had desired Peter to admit no one; but you know well that you, my dear son, are always an exception."

A pause ensued. Bertram looked at Gotzkowsky in an uneasy and searching manner, who was once more seated at his writing table, turning over his papers with a melancholy air.

Bertram had been absent nearly a year. The secret sorrow which day and night slowly gnawed his soul, had undermined his health and destroyed his physical strength. The physicians had pronounced a year's residence at Nice to be absolutely necessary; and when Bertram followed their advice, and went to Nice, he said to himself, "Perhaps Elise will think of me when I am gone; perhaps absence will make her heart beat more warmly for me; she may forget the brother, and one day welcome me as her husband." But when at the end of a year he returned renovated, and restored to health, he found Elise exactly as he had left her.

She received him in the same quiet, unexcited manner with which she had taken leave of him; she placed her hand in his in the same cool and friendly way, and, while she inquired after his health with cordial sympathy, Bertram felt that her heart and her inmost feelings had no share in her questions.

Elise had remained the same; but what a change in Gotzkowsky! Where was the enthusiastic strong willed man who had embraced him at parting? where was his clear ringing voice—his proud deportment—his energetic mind—his ardent eloquence? where were all these? What mysterious or diabolical power had succeeded in breaking this iron will?

Bertram felt convinced that some deep grief was poisoning Gotzkowsky's life; the more fatal because so carefully concealed. He resolved therefore to endeavour to obtain his confidence, convinced that in his sympathy his adopted father would at least find some consolation in sharing his burden with him.

He had intruded into Gotzkowsky's presence with the firm intention of carrying out this resolution, and now stood opposite to him looking with kind sympathy at his pale and sorrowful face. Gotzkowsky, however, carefully avoided meeting his eye; he appeared absorbed in his papers, and kept turning them over and examining them.

Bertram could bear it no longer: he hurried up to him, and, seizing his hand, pressed it respectfully to his lips.

"Father," said he, "forgive me! but when I look at you a vague fear oppresses me, for which I can scarcely account. You know I love you as truly as if you were my own father, and well can I read every expression of your countenance. I have, alas! discovered much care and anxiety in it since my return."

"Have you?" said Gotzkowsky sadly. "Yes, yes! grief is not written in hieroglyphics, it is a writing which all can understand."

"You own, then, that you have a sorrow, yet you conceal it from me?" asked Bertram eagerly. "You do not let me share your sorrows as I have done your joys. Father, have I deserved this?"

Gotzkowsky had risen from his chair and gone to the window with a thoughtful air and breathing heavily. For the first time he knew the blessing of sympathy from a kindred soul, and involuntarily the crust which had formed round his heart gave way before the voice of affection, and made him feel that he could not resist the young man's appeal. He turned to Bertram, and said in a gentle tone, "You are right, my son, I ought not to have hidden my anxieties from you; it will indeed be a comfort to me to impart them. Then hear what I have to say;—but no, first tell me what is rumoured of me in the city, and, above all, on the exchange? Ah! you cast down your eyes? Bertram, I must and will know all. Speak out freely, I have courage to hear the worst."

But his voice faltered, and his lips quivered convulsively. Bertram replied sorrowfully, "What need you care for the gossip of malicious people? you know that you have enemies because you are wealthy and noble-minded; you have long been envied because your house is the most solid and the most esteemed in all Germany; because your bills circulate everywhere, and are considered on the exchange of every country equal to solid gold. The jealousy caused by the fame of your firm, leads people to whisper and hint what they dare not say openly. What are their miserable insinuations to you?"

Bertram tried to smile, but it was a vain attempt, which did not escape Gotzkowsky's quick eye.

"Ah!" said he, "such low whispers of calumny resemble solitary snow flakes, which at length unite more and more till they form the mighty lawine, which will eventually bury beneath it our house and our good name. Tell me all, Bertram; what are these whispers?"

Bertram answered in a low, timid, hesitating voice, "It is said that your house has suffered enormous losses; that you are no longer in a condition to honour your bills; that your riches are only a chimera, and that—but" interrupting himself, "why should I repeat to you such old women's tales, such stupid newspaper reports?"

"The newspapers also speak of it?" said Gotzkowsky.

"Yes; the Voss newspaper has brought forth an article which contains a mysterious and compassionate allusion to the approaching failure of one of our greatest mercantile houses. People believe that yours is the house alluded to, father!"

"And the other paper—the Spenner?"

"Confirms to-day, with regret, this report."

Gotzkowsky burst into a mocking laugh; his face glowed with noble indignation, and his features resumed their former energy and resolution.

"Oh! world! oh! men!" said he; "how miserable and wretched ye are! You know, Bertram, how kind I was to both these men—I proved myself their friend in time of need—I saved them from insult and injury. In return for this they now hasten to trumpet forth my misfortunes to the world, and what is still hidden and denied by the kind consideration of my friends, and which indeed may yet be repaired, these ungrateful beihgs announce to the public, and thus hasten my fall."

"It is then but too true?" cried Bertram, turning pale; "you are in danger?"

"To-day is the last term of the liquidation of the 500,000 dollars which I engaged to pay our King for the city of Leipzig. Our principal banks bought up this debt of the King's from me."

"But it is not your own debt—you are only a guarantee for Leipzig."

"True; but, as Leipzig cannot pay, I must."

"Cannot Leipzig at least discharge part of her own debt?"

"Perhaps," said Gotzkowsky, thoughtfully; "I have sent a courier thither, and every moment I expect his return; but it is not that alone which distresses me," said he after a pause. "The 500,000 dollars would not be difficult to find, if other misfortunes had not occurred at the same moment. The new and most unexpected law about the coinage which was published yesterday, prohibiting the circulation of light coin, deprives me of half a million. As I anticipated Leipzig's inability to pay, I had negociated a loan of half a million of light gold with Hamburg, but spies of the Jews belonging to the Mint discovered this, and contrived, as soon as my money left Hamburg, to obtain an instant prohibition from the King for this sort of coin being available—thus my 500,000 dollars are good for nothing."*

"Dreadful, indeed!" cried Bertram; "but have you not tried to save at least a part of this large sum?"

* Biography of a Patriotic Merchant.

"I have," said Gotzkowsky, with a bitter laugh. "I tried more than once. I wished to send 50,000 of this money to the allied armies, to see if it would circulate there; but Ephraim had anticipated this also, and extorted an order that this light coin should not even pass anywhere through Prussia.* This new and capricious law was not, indeed, published till my money had left Hamburg, and I had hoped to bring it through Prussia unopposed, for it was concealed in the double lining of a carriage. But covetousness has sharp eyes, and the spies set to watch my every action succeeded in discovering this also. The carriage was stopped at the gates of Berlin, and they soon discovered—what, indeed, they already knew—the 50,000 dollars in the carriage. Who do you think, Bertram, came forward on this occasion to denounce me? You will never guess—the mayor, Kircheisen. He stood himself at the gate and watched till the carriage arrived, and never ceased searching it until he discovered the money."

* Gotzkowsky's Life, p. 188.

"Kircheisen!" cried Bertram; "not the same, father, whom you saved from death when the Russians were here?"

"The very same, my son. You shake your head dubiously—read this!"

He took from his writing-table a paper, to which was attached a large official seal, and gave it to Bertram.

"Read it yourself, my son—it is a rescript from the minister Von Finkenstein. See, there it stands: 'The president Von Kircheisen, by the King's decree, as discoverer and denouncer'* of the money, 'is to receive one-half of the sum.' A worthy title, 'discoverer and denouncer.' By heavens! I don't envy him that distinction. But you shall now know all," said he, after a pause; "it relieves me to throw myself on your sympathy, and it eases my poor heart to tell you my sorrows. Another fear tortures me: you have heard of my speculation with the Russian magazines?"

"Of the magazines which you purchased

* Biography of a Patriotic Merchant.

along with the bankers Moses and Samuel?" asked Bertram.

"Yes, just so; but Russia would not deliver up the contract till I became responsible for the whole sum."*

"And you did so?" asked Bertram, starting.

"I did. The purchase-money was due four months ago, and my fellow-contractors have not paid their share; so, if Russia presses her demands with severity, I am ruined."

"And why not call on Moses and Samuel for their share?" asked Bertram.

Gotzkowsky was silent for a moment, and, when he spoke, he said, in a tone of scorn and contempt, "Moses and Samuel are no longer obliged to pay, for they yesterday declared themselves bankrupts."

Bertram with difficulty suppressed a cry of rage, and covered his face with his hands. "He is lost!" murmured he, in a voice of anguish, "irretrievably lost! for he still clings to De Neufville as a last hope, and knows nothing as yet of his unhappy fate."

* Biography of a Patriotic Merchant.

## CONFESSIONS.

When Bertram once more looked up, Gotzkowsky was standing beside him, and gazing, with a sad and tender expression, at his distressed and horrified countenance. It was Gotzkowsky now who tried to inspire Bertram with confidence, while, with a calm, gentle smile, he related to him the hopes which still remained.

"De Neufville may return," said he, cheerfully; "he only went to the opening of the bank at Amsterdam, and if he succeeds in collecting the necessary sums there, and brings them to Berlin without delay, I shall be saved."

"But if he does not come?" asked Bertram, in a trembling voice, while fixing his anxious looks searchingly on Gotzkowsky.

"Then I must be irretrievably ruined," cried Gotzkowsky, in an excited voice.

Bertram threw himself into his arms, and pressed him to his heart, as if wishing to shelter him there, and to shield him from all the impending misery.

"You must be saved," said he, eagerly; "it is not possible that you should sink—you have not deserved such a misfortune."

"For that very reason am I doomed to suffer so deeply," said Gotzkowsky, with a heavy sigh. "If I had deserved this shame probably it never would have befallen me. The world is so constituted, that men seldom receive their deserts here below, whether for good or evil."

"But you have friends," said Bertram; "thousands are bound to testify their gratitude to you for your magnanimity, and the aid you have so often bestowed on them. There is scarcely a single merchant in Berlin whom you have not in one way or in another assisted in time of difficulty and danger."

Gotzkowsky said sorrowfully,

"My young friend, those very men who owe me most will be the first to destroy me—precisely the debt of gratitude they have incurred makes them my bitter enemies; for it is the nature of men rather to forgive the injuries they have received, than the benefits which have proved their salvation. The duty of gratitude is such a difficult virtue to practise, that men invariably become the irreconcileable foes of those who have imposed this burden on them."

"When you speak thus, father," cried Bertram glowing with noble indignation, "you include me also in the base number of ingrates. You have bound me to everlasting gratitude by your innumerable benefits, and I still love you devotedly."

"You form a singular exception," said Gotzkowsky gravely; "but I thank God that you do so."

Bertram looked at him earnestly.

"You place faith in me, then," said he.

"I do believe firmly in your truth," said Gotzkowsky solemnly

"Well, then, my dear father," cried Bertram joyfully, "allow me to ask you one last favour in this decisive hour. You call me your son, grant me the privileges of one—bestow the happiness on me of seeing you accept the sacrifice of the little I possess. My property is not indeed sufficient to be of material service to you; but it may at all events be of some use. To you, father, I owe all I possess—it is your own, receive it back from me."

"Never!" interrupted Gotzkowsky firmly.

But Bertram continued more impetuously,

"Take it into consideration at all events. When you founded your porcelain manufactory, you made me a partner in the speculation, and I accepted the benefit, though I had nothing in the world but what you gave me. When the King bought the fabric from you a year ago,* you apportioned to me nearly one fourth

* The King purchased the china manufactory from Gotzkowsky in August, 1763, for 125,000 dollars, and showed the greatest interest in it. To promote the sale, the King issued an edict in 1769, by which the Jews for every pass of protection, and every concession, must purchase 300 dollars' worth of china from the royal manufactory. The lottery office keepers were also obliged to buy 10,000 dollars' worth of porcelain.

of the purchase-money, and paid me down 30,000 dollars. I received it from you thankfully, though I had not contributed the smallest capital towards it."

"You are wrong, my son; you forget the industry and the talent with which you enriched the business and made it prosper."

"Talent is no capital," cried Bertram reluctantly; "I might have starved with all my knowledge, if you had not nobly adopted me. Therefore, father, take back your own, I implore of you, and receive the money."

Gotzkowsky made a strong gesture of dissent, and Bertram continued more eagerly,

"Father, if I were in truth your son, would you deny me the right at least to share your ruin? Could you refuse your son when offering to share with you all he possessed?"

"No," cried Gotzkowsky; "on the contrary, I would expect this sacrifice from a son of my own; for it is not only worldly wealth which is at stake, but the holiest possession of any man —the honour of my name. Had I a son, I would expect that he should even go to death with me, if by so doing he could rescue my good name and my credit."

"In that case," said Bertram, "let me become in truth your son—give me your daughter."

Gotzkowsky started and gazed at Bertram's glowing noble countenance.

"Ah!" cried he, "you are a high-souled man, Bertram, and I thank you. I can penetrate your motives. You have discovered what most of all poisons and agonises my heart—that my child will become a beggar by my ruin: you nobly come to her rescue, and will shield her from want and penury."

"No, father, I would fain see her mine because I truly love her," cried Bertram, "and I wish to be your son to acquire the right to give up all I have to you, and thus to have the privilege of working for you. Ah! you have, during the whole course of your life, done so much for others, grant me the happiness of now doing something for you—give me your daughter, and thus let me become your son."

Gotzkowsky seemed overcome with emotion, and, after a pause, he said solemnly,

"You know that this has always been a favourite project of mine; but what I have so truly wished during many long years I must now decline—I cannot bear to involve you in my misfortunes; and, even were I so weak as to yield to your entreaties, I dare not sacrifice the happiness of my daughter for my own benefit. Do you sincerely think, Bertram, that Elise loves you?"

"She likes me, and feels an interest in my welfare—that is sufficient," said Bertram, in a low tone; "through many a year of suffering I have learned to give up all hope of her love."

"But if Elise loves another? I fear her heart is only too faithful, and that she has not yet forgotten the villain who destroyed her happiness. When I think of that man anger and contempt fill my soul. At the hour of death I will forgive all my enemies; but my hatred of the man who trifled with the love and trust of my child I will carry with me to the grave; and yet I much fear that my Elise has never forgotten him."

"These smouldering memories, this dead

love, do not disquiet me," said Bertram; "four years have elapsed since that day—"

"And four long years I have faithfully hated him," interrupted Gotzkowsky. "May not, therefore, Elise have loved him as faithfully during all that period?"

Bertram sighed and cast down his eyes mournfully.

"It is but too true," said he, "love does not die so quickly——Father," continued he resolutely, after a short pause, "I repeat my request—bestow your daughter on me."

"You know that she does not love you, and yet you wish to marry her."

"Yes, I ask you for her hand," said Bertram; "I feel so much confidence in Elise, that I know she will not reject me when she learns that you will not accept of my small means unless I become your son. She will joyfully make this sacrifice for her father's sake. Her love for you will induce her to give me her hand, and thus to obtain for me the privileges of your son."

"Never!" cried Gotzkowsky, impetuously,

"never shall she know what we have just said. She is quite ignorant as yet of the misfortunes which are impending over her. I have not courage to tell her of them; indeed, why should I do so? When the worst comes to pass, she will know it quite soon enough; and, if it can be averted, the evil hour will have passed over her unheeded. For my child a clear and pure sky, for me clouds and storms! This has been the great aim of my life, and I will continue it to the end."

"You are determined to reject me," said Bertram, with tears in his eyes.

"No, my son," said Gotzkowsky, affectionately, "I accept what you have just offered me, the treasure of your love; that I never can lose—if the world deprives me of all else, that will always be mine."

Both remained silent, but their troubled souls sympathised, and they understood each other without words or assurances of love.

At last Gotzkowsky spoke—his voice was calm and his air almost cheerful.

"I thank you, Bertram," said he, "you have

inspired me with fresh courage and resolution —I will resume all my presence of mind, humble my pride, and have recourse to those who vowed everlasting gratitude to me in former days. The magistrates of Berlin still owe me 20,000 ducats from the time when the Russians were in Berlin. Moreover, I was obliged to make two journeys from Berlin to Petersburg and Warsaw on their affairs. They have never paid the sums I expended at that time—I shall take the liberty of reminding them of it now. Come, Bertram, let us go together to these gentlemen, and see if they have any recollection of all the sacred assurances they uttered of love and gratitude, when they required help, and were threatened by misfortune."

## THE RUSSIAN PRINCE.

A DUSTY travelling carriage stopped at the door of one of the first hotels in Berlin. The team of six horses, and the two servants on the box, denoted that the traveller who intended to honour the hotel by his presence, must be a person of distinction. It was therfore very natural that the landlord should hurry out to receive him, and, with a respectful bow, open the door of his carriage.

A tall, slender, young man descended with a languid, haughty air from his equipage; and, while passing slowly and silently into the house, he asked his French courier whether the landlord had any tolerable apartments, sufficiently brilliant and well furnished to receive Prince Stratimojeff.

The face of the landlord was brightened by a satisfied smile; he hurriedly snatched the candelabra from the head waiter, and rushed up stairs with it himself, to throw open the state apartments of his house for the reception of the Prince.

The courier examined the suite of rooms with a critical eye, and pronounced them, if not fully equal to his master's pretensions, at least sufficiently good to receive his Highness, who was following them up stairs.

The Prince was still silent, his travelling cap crushed down on his forehead, and his whole figure closely wrapped in a wide fur cloak which reached to the ground.

He made a sign to the landlord with a silent gesture to leave the room, then in a few short words desired his valet to order dinner for him, and to serve it in the adjoining room; and, as at this moment another carriage drove up to the door, he told the servant to go to the window and see if it was his suite arriving. The valet reported that it was the train of his Highness—his private secretary, agent, and chaplain.

"I do not want to see them again to-day,"

said the Prince imperiously. "They may do what they choose; but tell them that to-morrow our business must begin; as for you, Guillaume, I have an important commission which I wish you to execute. First of all you must inquire from the landlord about the rich banker Gotzkowsky, and, when you have found out where he lives, continue the conversation, and try to obtain all the information you can about him and his affairs. I wish to ascertain every particular about his family. You must ask about the daughter, and whether she is still unmarried, and if she resides in Berlin; in short, you will endeavour to find out all you can about the family."

The obsequious valet had left the room for a considerable time, and yet Prince Stratimojeff was still standing on the same spot, absorbed apparently in a reverie, and only muttering occasionally a few indistinct words.

Suddenly he threw off from his shoulders the wide fur cloak in which he was enveloped, and flung his cap on a sofa.

"Air! air!" cried he. "I feel as if I were

suffocating. The aspect of this city oppresses me with the weight of lead, and like a criminal I would fain hide myself from all men."

He tore open his coat and breathed heavily, his brow was thoughtful and troubled, his lips firmly compressed.

What was it which caused Prince Stratimojeff such violent emotion, and made his whole frame tremble as from fever? It was the remembrance of former days, the accusing and torturing voice of conscience which agonised him thus.

Why did Prince Stratimojeff occupy himself with the affairs of the banker Gotzkowsky and his daughter? Could the heart of Graf Féodor von Brenda have grown so hard that he did not care, when he returned to Berlin, to hear of her whom he had once so shamefully deceived?

It was he!—Féodor von Brenda had been transformed into Prince Stratimojeff—but what devastation have those four short years made in his inmost life! They have been four years of dissolute pleasure, of enervating folly; four years of bacchanalism, luxury, of intoxication of the senses, which the count had passed in the court of two Russian empresses. Elizabeth had died in the meantime, and the unhappy Peter the Third had worn only for a few short days the Russian crown. It was too heavy for his weak head, and his illustrious consort Katherine, full of compassion and Russian humanity, had endeavoured to lighten the burden for him—only, in her too great zeal, she had taken off not only the crown, but the head along with it, and changed the unhappy Emperor's prison into a grave.

The guards shouted for the new empress as they had done for the former one. In the presence of the beautiful young Empress Katherine, they remembered with delight that the Empress Elizabeth had been always such a gracious condescending mistress, that, in the plenitude of her goodness and power, she transformed noncommissioned officers into princes, and common soldiers into great nobles. Why, therefore, should not Katherine be equally discerning towards her handsome soldiers of the Guards?

She was gracious—she was a kind mistress to all her subjects, but more especially so to the handsome men in her kingdom; and Graf Féodor von Brenda was a peculiarly handsome man. He had been the favourite of the Empress Elizabeth. Why should he not be the favourite also of the Empress Katherine? The former had conferred on him her maternal tenderness, for she was old; Katherine, however, was young, and in her proud breast a fiery heart glowed, which included more than one among her favourites and lovers.

For some short months Féodor von Brenda was the declared favourite of the empress, and every one did him homage, and thought it very natural that Katherine should elevate him to the rank of Prince Stratimojeff, and not only bestow stars and orders and titles on him, but also magnificent properties and thousands of serfs. What a strange, happy, intoxicating life was his; how all the world envied the handsome, wealthy prince enjoying the brightest rays of imperial favour!

But, nevertheless, a heavy cloud was always on his forehead, and he rushed into the sea of dissipation like one in a fever, who seeks to cool the fire which is inwardly consuming him. He threw himself recklessly into the arms of pleasure, like a criminal condemned to death, who madly spends the last hours of his life in the excitement of champagne, striving to forget that Death stands behind him, and already extends his skeleton hand to clutch him for his own.

Thus Féodor also tried, in the giddy whirl of sensuality, to drown his thoughts and to deaden his feelings; but there were quiet hours which reminded him of the past, and sometimes he started from his couch and listened, for he thought he heard once more a faint scream, a heart breaking cry which penetrated his very soul; but this solitary cry was only the echo of his dream, in which he saw Elise's pale and sorrowing face, and he trembled at the despair he saw impressed on that sweet countenance. Beside this ethereal shape sometimes appeared another pale woman, whose anguished looks martyrised him, and he felt, with a shudder, that he saw before him Lodoiska von Sandomir, whose gloomy and saddened aspect seemed to demand from him the murdered happiness of her youth and life.

She died—grief killed her; for she felt that the man to whom she had sacrificed herself, had never forgiven her for separating him from Elise, and becoming his wife by exercising a deception.

She died from his contempt, neglect, and hatred.

Scorn on his part did not kill her like a flash of lightning, but slowly and surely penetrated into her soul, and poisoned her life. During one miserable, lonely year she bore this martyrdom, and then she died a solitary death. No loving hand dried the drops of anguish on her pale brow; no compassionate lips whispered words of love, and the bright hope to meet again in a better world; but her heart was not yet hardened to her husband and the lover of her youth, and even on her death-bed she invoked blessings on his head.

This was proved by the touching letter, full of humble love and forgiving tenderness, which the Prince, her husband, found on his writing table, and which she had written with trembling fingers, already paralysed by the near approach of death. There was another letter, too, addressed to Elise Gotzkowsky.

Lodoiska had loved her husband well enough to know the cause of his dissolute life. She knew that in the depths of his heart he still mourned over the only true love he had ever felt, the love for Elise, and that the dissipations he indulged in were despairing and vain attempts to stifle the sorrows of his heart. Elise's image followed him everywhere, and the love which might have proved the blessing of his existence had become an oppressive curse to the guilty man.

In the midst of the wildest revelry, during the secret imperial orgies, her image started up before him, like a guardian angel, and made him suddenly silent, quelling the arrogant jest on his quivering lips, and an inward voice seemed to say, "Fly to Elise, with her alone is peace and rest. If you can still be saved she will save you."

But he had not strength of mind to follow

the warning voice of his troubled conscience; he was fettered by golden links, and, though not those of love, yet pride and vanity still enthralled him, and prevented his casting off his chains.

He was the avowed favourite of the young Empress, and the great nobles of the land eagerly cultivated his society, and were enchanted by a smile from him, or a pressure of his hand. But everything in this world is full of change and uncertainty. The heart of the Empress Katherine had also undergone a transformation.

One day Prince Stratimojeff received a note from his royal mistress, in which she proposed to him a diplomatic mission to Germany, and requested him, on account of the urgency of the affair, to set off on his journey without delay.

Féodor at once comprehended the secret meaning of this apparently gracious and tender note; he knew that he had lost her favour, not from having committed any fault, but simply because Count Orloff was handsomer and more attractive than himself, or at least appeared so in the Empress's eyes.

On this account Féodor's vicinity was disagreeable, and she wished to remove him; for at that time—the beginning of her reign—Katherine had at least so much sense of shame that favouritism was not a declared Court office, but still considered as a secret; which, however, all knew.

At that period she wished to avoid the dismissed favourite being brought into contact with his successor, and thus she commanded Féodor to set off for Germany, before openly replacing him by Graf Alexis Orloff.

Féodor crushed the perfumed imperial note in his hand, and muttered between his teeth, "She has sacrificed me to Orloff. She wishes to get rid of me, to display this new bauble of her love undisturbed. Well! I go! but never more to return to her, to allow myself again to be fooled by her gracious looks and protestations of attachment. No; this breach between us is irreparable. Katherine shall feel that she is only a woman, whom I despise, although she is an Empress. Not the least word of farewell, not the slightest remonstrance on my part. She bids me go, and I go at once. And does it not seem as if Fate herself pointed out to me the path I should follow? Is it not a marvellous chance that Katherine should herself despatch me on this mission to Germany?"

It was, indeed, a strange coincidence that Katherine, without knowing it, should send the lover of whom she was weary, to her whom alone Féodor had ever truly loved.

The Empress despatched Féodor as a special envoy to Berlin, to give more weight to her injunctions to a Prussian banker, to sue at law the merchant Johann Gotzkowsky for his debt to Russia of two millions of dollars, and, if he delayed payment, to endeavour by diplomatic means to persuade the Prussian Government to support her claim, and to enforce her rights.

This was the mission which Katherine had entrusted to Prince Stratimojeff; but, while he resolved to accept it, he said to himself, "I will be revenged on this haughty, faithless woman, who thinks she can cast me aside like a plaything of which she is weary. I will show her that my heart is quite unmoved by her want of fidelity. I will present my lovely young wife to her, before whose beauty, youth, and innocence she shall cast down her eyes and blush."

Animated with such purposes he went to the last supper party of the Empress. There was yet one evening of gaiety and dissipation for him before his journey commenced, and he was resolved to make this evening a triumph, and a medium of revenge for his wrongs. Never, therefore, had he been so brilliant, so witty, so amiable, so gay, as on this night. His jests were the boldest, the most daring; they even caused the Empress almost to regret his loss.

The Court had rejoiced beforehand, in the hope of seeing the long-envied and hated, but now humbled and disgraced, favourite replaced on this evening by the new minion; but they saw with surprise and disappointment that the expected humiliation was changed into a triumph for Féodor, for the Empress, fascinated by his wit and agreeability, seemed once more to restore her heart to him, and by her tender glances to entreat forgiveness for her caprice.

She would fain now have dismissed from her thoughts the unlucky embassy which was to remove Féodor from her Court, but he reminded her of it himself.

While all faces were beaming with delight at Féodor's flow of sarcasm and wit, which seemed to especially enchant the Empress, he went up to her and begged for her good wishes on his journey, which he was to undertake that very night. Katherine would gladly have recalled her command, but she was woman enough to penetrate through the disguise of gaiety he had assumed, and to read in his face the scorn and indignation he really felt. She therefore simply entreated him to return as speedily as he could.

Then publicly, before the whole assembled Court and her new favourite, she granted one more triumph to Prince Stratimojeff. She desired him to kneel down before her, and hung a gold chain round his neck, to which was suspended her own portrait. She touched his forehead lightly with her lips, and said with a gracious and kind smile, "Adieu, au revoir."

## OLD LOVE AND NEW SORROW.

Elise was in her room, in the same state of quiet composure and indifference as usual. Her large dark eyes had a sorrowful but calm expression. She was seated in an arm-chair reading; and as she sat there her noble and regular features, her lofty forehead, and her beautifully chiselled lips, gave her the appearance of one of those highly favoured beings whom Heaven has gifted with undisturbed peace and cheerfulness, and who has never tasted the bitter cup of suffering.

There was no trace now of any of the storms which had raged at one time in her existence. Her grief had spent itself inwardly. Her gaiety of spirit was blighted for ever, but her face had remained young and lovely. Her youthful strength of constitution had conquered the sorrows of her soul; and her cheeks, though colourless and of almost transparent paleness, were not tinged with that sickly yellow hue which usually presages early death.

She was young and lovely outwardly, but sad and suffering within. Probably her frozen heart only required one bright ray of sunshine again to melt in tenderness—only one gleam of hope to renew the youth of her soul, and its strength once more to love and to suffer.

She had never forgotten the past—never had she ceased to think of him whom she had once so ardently loved, and to whose memory she still fondly clung; reminiscences of other days formed the sole thoughts and occupation of the present.

The trees in the garden which he had once admired, the flowers which he loved, and which had since then four times in early springing youth renewed their fragrant blossoms, the rustling of the firs which was borne to her on the breezes from near the garden palings he had once sprung over to see her, and to bid her a long adieu—all these things reminded her of him, and made her heart beat, she scarcely herself knew whether with joy or sorrow.

Even at this moment, when she was seated in her room, her thoughts and dreams were all busy with the past. She had been reading, but the book had fallen from her listless hand. From the love scenes depicted there, her thoughts had strayed to the far and distant past, recalling many hopes now blighted for ever, many fond reveries never to be realised.

But Elise did not wish to yield to these temptations to linger on the bitter past; she dreaded her own thoughts, and was unwilling to confess even to herself that she still loved the man who had so cruelly deceived her.

She leant her head wearily on the chair, and her large dark eyes gazed into empty space. Some particular passage in the book had reminded her of her own unfortunate passion—vibrating on her heart as the hammer does on the bell, and it had responded with the one word —"Féodor!" Her pale cheeks flushed when she uttered this name. "Ah!" said she softly, "my lips to-day for the first time utter this word, but my soul has often breathed it in despairing misery, and he has lived for me in my dreams. I have accepted my sad fate. I had strength of will to be separated from him outwardly; but inwardly—never. Ah! how mysterious is the human heart! I hate him, and yet—I love him too."

She covered her face with her hands, and sat long silent and motionless. A knock at the door aroused her; it was Marianne, her maid, who came to say that a stranger was without, who was very urgent in his wish to see her.

Elise trembled, and scarcely knew why a painful presentiment shot through her soul, as she asked, in a scarcely audible voice, the name of the gentleman.

"He will not give it," answered the girl; "he says that his name is of no consequence. He has been charged to deliver a message to you from Gräfin Lodoiska in Petersburg."

Elise uttered a sharp cry, and started up; she knew all—her heart foreboded his vicinity—it must be Féodor himself, and no other, who was without.

She felt an irresistible impulse to fly to her father, and find refuge and safety with him.

But her feet refused to bear her to him; she shook from head to foot, and was obliged to cling to the back of a chair to prevent herself sinking to the ground; she made a silent gesture of dissent, but Marianne not comprehending her opened the door, ushered in the stranger, and left the room.

They stood face to face, breathless and silent. Elise trembling from emotion and outraged love; Féodor struggling with his own agitation, and humiliated at the sight of the fair being whom he had so deeply wronged.

Both prayed inwardly: but how different was the tenor of their prayers!

"May an angel, or a spirit of evil," thought Féodor, "give my words power, and impart magic influence to my speech, so that I may win back my Elise once more!"

Elise prayed fervently, "Mercy, oh! Father, mercy! crush this unhallowed love of mine, or let me die!"

It was a dreary pause which ensued between those two beings who had been so long and fatally severed; both shuddered visibly—one from consciousness of his crime, the other from remorse at the continued existence of her love.

But at last he summoned courage to break the ominous silence. He whispered her name softly; and when she, startled and trembling with emotion at the accents of his much loved voice, looked up at him, he extended his arms to her imploringly; she felt, she thought, she knew nothing, save that he was before her. She uttered a low cry, and started forwards with the impulse to throw herself into his arms: but suddenly they both stopped short—the dream was dissolved, and, awaking from the first joy of seeing her lover once more, Elise shrunk back and drew herself up in all the pride and dignity of her wounded honour.

She had sufficient courage to suppress her first fond impulse, and, bending with cold and constrained politeness to Féodor, she asked, "Count von Brenda, who do you want here?"

The Prince sighed heavily, and dropped his extended arms. "It is all over," murmured he in a low tone, "she no longer loves me!"

But though these words were only whispered,

Elise had heard them, and they made her heart beat wildly.

"Whom do you seek here?" repeated she, in a faltering voice.

"No one now," said he, sadly; "I have been in error—I thought I might venture to seek a faithful heart, an angel, who, in the hour of reunion, forgetting all else, would take refuge in my arms and forgive the past, and remove, by her pardon, the curse which rests on my life. This was what I looked for; but God is just; I have not deserved such happiness, and I submit with resignation to His decrees."

"Ah!" said Elise to herself, "it is the same voice to which I once so loved to listen." She no longer found strength to bid him quit her presence; she would have given her life's blood to have seen him always thus near her.

"I come now, Mademoiselle Gotzkowsky," said Féodor, "only as a messenger, as one fulfilling the will of the dead." He took a letter from his breast and gave it to Elise: "I bring you a letter written just before her death by my late wife, Gräfin Lodoiska," said he, solemnly.

"She no longer lives?" cried Elise, and almost unconsciously a tone of relief pervaded her words.

This did not escape Prince Stratimojeff. "I shall win her at last," said he, mentally; his eyes beamed, and a feeling of proud triumphant joy made his heart beat violently.

Elise had taken the letter, and held it hesitatingly in her hand.

"Will you not read it?" said he, in a low tone; and the imploring sound of his voice made her shiver with emotion.

"I will read it," said she, appearing to wake out of a dream, and breaking the seal hastily.

The Prince fixed his watchful glance on her, wishing to read her inmost thoughts, and, seeing with delight that they seemed relenting towards him, he drew nearer to her.

The letter was short and hurriedly written, but every word found a response in Elise's soul, and brought tears to her eyes.

It ran thus—

"My dear Elise, when you receive this I shall be no more, and the heart which has suffered so much will have ceased to beat and to grieve; but, if I am to find rest in the grave, I entreat you to fulfil my last wish. I bequeath to you the dearest object I have on earth. I restore a possession which has never ceased to be your own—the love and the heart of Féodor. I have failed in gaining his love. He gave me his hand, but his heart has always been yours—and this has caused my death. Take him from my hands as a sacred legacy, and, when you meet again, my purified spirit will bless your reunion.—LODOISKA."

The paper dropped from Elise's hand. Quite overpowered by deep and holy emotion, she sunk down on a couch, and covered her weeping face with her hands.

Féodor felt that she was once more his own, and that his power over her would soon be as great as ever. He rushed up to her, and, kneeling at her feet, removed by gentle force her hands from her face, and said with passionate emotion—

"Elise, her spirit is at this moment hovering near us. She consecrates our love, which she has long forgiven. Oh! if you knew what I have suffered from your loss, you would at least be softened towards me; you would forgive me for the sake of all I have endured."

"And have I not then suffered?" asked she, turning her eyes fondly on him, dimmed by tears.

"Oh! let me remain here at your feet," continued he. "Consider me as a poor pilgrim, wandering to the Holy Sepulchre. May I lay my sorrows on your shrine, and pour out my griefs and anguish before you?"

"Speak on," said she, half unconscious, her ear drinking in the melody of his much loved voice; "tell me what you have endured, that I may forget my own misery when forced to give you up."

"Oh!" said he, with a shudder, "never can I forget the dreadful moment when I became aware of the agonising deception, and discovered that I was holding Lodoiska in my arms, and not you. A mad fury—which I wished to wreak on my own life—seized me; but Lodoiska arrested the dagger in my hand by uttering your name. That dear name recalled me to life, and to the consciousness of my guilt. I submitted to the punishment of my crime which you had imposed on me. I led Lodoiska to the altar. I made her my wife; but my heart cherished your dear image, even at the moment when my lips pronounced the marriage vows to another. It was a fearful hour. Constant anguish undermined my health, and poisoned my very existence. Only when death was near—when in the heat of battle the cannons of the foe raged around me—did I feel happy or excited, and rushed into the ranks of the enemy in the hope of meeting death—but death itself rejected me. I won honour and fame on the field of battle—the only thing I could not win, was death. I lived to suffer on, and to repent bitterly my treachery towards you, my Elise There was but one hope which sustained me—that of one day throwing myself at your feet to implore your forgiveness."

Quite overpowered by his own vivid delineation of all his misery, the Prince's voice faltered. He had succeeded in moving his own feelings, and really believed in his own sorrows. He had so entirely adopted the tone of a repentant sinner, and an ardent lover, that his feelings became almost truth and reality, and penetrated his soul with passionate grief.

Elise, however, believed him. The tender accents of his voice made every fibre of her heart vibrate. The past, with its sorrows and trials, was forgotten—he was once more at her feet—the shadow of no betrothed bride now interposed to sever them, and she only felt that she loved him as fondly as ever.

He clasped his hands, and looked up at her imploringly.

"Elise," said he, "only forgive me! Speak but the word of pardon, and I will leave you at once, and never again dare to approach you."

Elise had no longer strength to resist him. "Féodor," said she, tenderly, "love does not forgive—no, it only loves on," and tears of inexpressible happiness streamed over her cheeks.

Féodor uttered a cry of joy, and sprang up to clasp her in his arms, covering her blushing face with kisses, and whispering words of delight and passionate love into her willing ear.

"Oh!" said he, "all is well again—once more you are mine—my own!—the last four miserable years are blotted out—it was only an evil dream which has for ever passed away—we know now how truly we love, and that we must belong to each other—come, my Elise, it is the same hour which once before called us to the bridal altar—the priest awaits us; come, my darling."

But Elise shook her head, and said softly, "The shade of Lodoiska no longer severs us; but my father! without his blessing never will I consent to quit my home. God saw fit to punish us before, because we had not implored the sanction of a parent. I had sadly failed in duty towards him—this has been bitterly atoned for—destiny is reconciled; let us go hand in hand to my father and entreat his consent to our union, and to the love which has endured through long years of anguish, and will last beyond death—even to eternity."

There was something so ardent and so inspired in her whole being, that Féodor felt involuntarily carried away by her enthusiasm.

"I submit to your will in all things," said he humbly; "your wishes are mine; but will not your father angrily repel me? I feel that he must hate me for the tears I have made you shed!"

"He will love you when he sees that I have learned to smile again for your sake," said she. "Let us go to him."

She wished to lead him gently with her, but his conscience-stricken soul held him back—he had not the audacity to face the man whose ruin he had come expressly to insure, and involuntarily he trembled at his own deeds.

"I dare not present myself so unprepared before him!" said he, hesitating.

"Then at least allow me to inform him that you are here?"

"And if he refuses his consent?"

"He will not refuse."

"He solemnly vowed never to give you to a Russian."

"Oh! that was in other times," said she,

smiling, "when the Russians were our enemies; now we are at peace—sanguinary streams no longer flow, and the angel of peace flies through every land; my father too will feel his holy influence, and be at peace with you and with me."

Féodor did not immediately answer—he stood pensive and absorbed, weighing in his mind what was best to be done; one thing alone was clear, neither Elise nor Gotzkowsky must be made aware of the singular mission with which the Empress had entrusted him. When Elise was irrevocably bound to him, and her father had given his consent to their union, then, and not till then, would he perform the difficult task of being candid with Gotzkowsky.

It was therefore imperative to delay for a time all negociation about the demands for the Russian subsidy—he must give his agent the necessary instructions forthwith, and desire him to preserve entire secrecy for another day.

The chief thing was to persuade Elise and her father that the proposed marriage should take place immediately, as his stay in Berlin was necessarily limited to a few hours.

He placed his arm round Elise's slender waist, and pressed her fondly to his heart. "Hear me, my beloved!" said he, impetuously, "the time doled out to me is short—I came hither with courier's horses, to gain a few hours longer stay here before recommencing my journey; but we must set off this very night, for the army is still assembled, and ready for offensive operations at the boundaries of the empire; and only as a mark of distinguished favour did the Empress Katherine grant me a short leave for the purpose of fetching my bride. She has graciously done all she could, and I must obey her commands by a speedy return, if I am not prepared to bring the extremity of her wrath on my head. That nothing might prevent or delay our marriage, I have brought with me a chaplain of our Church to consecrate our union. You see therefore my own Elise that all is prepared, and that nothing is wanting but the myrtle wreath in your hair."

"And the blessing of my father," said she, gravely.

Féodor frowned, and a gloomy expression

crossed his face. Elise did not see it, for, in happy self forgetfulness, she had leant her head on his shoulder, and her fond love was incapable of doubt or mistrust.

A woman who loves is of a celestial nature. She pardons all, she suffers all; she is as lavish in giving as in forgiving. Every woman who truly loves is for the time an inspired poetess,—a Godlike inspiration breathes over her soul. It was so with this poor girl. She leant fondly and trustingly on the man whom she had never ceased to love, whom she had never ceased to bless, even amid all the bitter tears she had shed for his sake,—for whom she had fervently prayed at the very time when his treachery had wrung her heart, and caused her in anguish of mind to implore the mercy of Providence.

"Go, then, to your father," said Féodor, after a pause. "Entreat for his consent, and his blessing on us both. In the meantime I hasten away to make the necessary preparations. Say to your father that my whole life shall pass in the endeavour to purchase by a smile, every tear which your dear eyes ever shed for my sake. Say to him that I will love him like a son, who receives from him life's fairest possession—yourself, my darling Elise!"

Elise looked up at him with a fond, confiding smile; but he placed his hand on her eyes,—he was not sufficiently hardened to endure their innocent, confiding expression.

"I must away," said he; "but this shall be our last separation; when I return, it will be for the purpose of leading you to the altar. You must be ready, my beloved, in two hours from this time, when I will come to claim my bride, and from thence we go straight to Petersburg, to present to the Empress and to her court my fair wife, Princess Stratimojeff."

He looked at her eagerly, wishing to see the impression his words would make. He had hoped to surprise her agreeably by this unexpected announcement of his new rank, and to see her blush from proud satisfaction; but Elise neither felt elevated nor honoured by this lofty title. What cared she whether Féodor were a prince or a poor officer, provided that he loved her, and would never more leave her!

She therefore only said, in a voice of surprise, "Princess Stratimojeff! What do you mean?"

"I have been for the last three months Prince Stratimojeff," answered he, with a proud smile. "The Empress bestowed this title on me. The world calls me Prince, but you, my own love, you will always call me your Féodor?"

"Ah!" said she, fondly, "my heart called you so, even when you were no longer mine."

"Farewell, dearest!" said he, tenderly embracing her. "Place the myrtle bridal wreath in your glossy hair, and in two hours expect my return."

He hurried to the door to depart; but on the threshold he turned once more, to wave her a parting adieu. She was standing on the same spot, and gazing after him. Their eyes met in a loving glance. Suddenly an unaccountable but deep emotion seized him. He had a feeling that he might never see her again

R 2

—that, if he once crossed the threshold, Elise would be lost to him for ever.

Once more he rushed back, and pressed her to his heart; and, quite overpowered by the painful presentiment which agitated his heart, he leant his head on her shoulder, and tears dimmed his eyes. Then he tore himself suddenly from her.

"Farewell!" said he, and his voice sounded loud and harsh; "farewell! In two short hours I return to fetch you. Be prepared, and do not let me wait a second time in vain. Farewell!"

## THE MAGISTRATES OF BERLIN.

Gotzkowsky had vanquished his proud heart. He had left his own house to repair to those, whose benefactor he had been in days of necessity and danger, and who had then vowed everlasting gratitude towards him. He was resolved now, though with a reluctant heart, to remind them of those days, and to ask of them, not assistance or favours, but simply payment of their just debts.

First of all he went to the President Kircheisen—the man whom he had saved from death when the Russians were in Berlin, when the worthy mayor had sworn one day to prove to Gotzkowsky his deep sense of all he owed him, saying he would bless the hour which enabled him to prove his gratitude by deeds. This hour had now arrived, but Herr von

Kircheisen no longer blessed it; on the contrary, he was more inclined to curse it.

He was standing at the window of a room on the ground floor when Gotzkowsky passed. Their eyes met; Gotzkowsky's were clear and searching, but Kircheisen cast down his, turned pale, and stepped back from the window. He had only just time to say to the servant that he was not at home to any one, when the door bell was heard, and Gotzkowsky inquired for the Mayor.

"Not at home, sir."

"Not at home? I saw him standing at the window this minute."

"You must be mistaken, sir; the president is at the Town Hall."

"Very well; in that case I will also go there," said Gotzkowsky.

As he again passed the window he looked in, but this time Herr von Kircheisen was no longer standing behind the panes of glass, but, half hidden by a curtain, cautiously peeping at Gotzkowsky through the window. As he saw him passing along, his face pallid and worn, and his figure bent by care, he involuntarily felt a degree of remorse, and his conscience reminded him of the debt yet undischarged, which he still owed to the man who had once saved his life.

But Herr von Kircheisen turned a deaf ear to this reminding voice; he frowned, and said to himself, with a sneer, "He is evidently bankrupt; I will have nothing to do with him."

So saying he went into his business room, and, yielding to a natural instinct, he opened his strong box and revelled in the sight of the thousands which he had earned as "a discoverer and denouncer" against Gotzkowsky. His conscience now no longer reproached him, the aspect of the dazzling glitter of the gold had entirely hushed it to rest.

In the meantime Gotzkowsky pursued his painful and humiliating pilgrimage. His mind was deeply depressed and full of anxious cares.

How many bitter and grievous experiences he made while passing along the streets! He met men who usually bowed to the ground before him, and on this day they scarcely noticed him; others in passing whispered with a malicious smile the word "bankrupt!" At the corner of a street he suddenly came in contact with Kretschmer, who was turning from another street. He came rather violently in collision with Gotzkowsky, but did not think it worth while to apologize; he only pressed his hat over his brows, and passed on with a glance of contempt.

As Gotzkowsky was going along he heard windows opening, and he knew that his former dear friends were eagerly looking after him, sneering at him, and ridiculing his unhappy position. It was, indeed, a spiritual mode of running the gauntlet. Gotzkowsky's soul bled from its effects, and his feet were languid and weary.

What had he done to deserve the scoffs and insults of the world? Had he not always been benevolent and hospitable, humane and philanthropic, kind and loving to all men? Had he not conferred benefits on others without ever expecting any return?

His faults and his crimes were his independence. He had never sought for favour from his fellow men—relying on himself alone, he had always built on his own strength.

His fellow citizens now wished to make him feel that he had wounded their pride by being so self existent ; for petty natures never pardon any man for presuming to be free and to act for themselves, and, instead of being indebted to others for their prosperity, to owe no thanks save to themselves.

Now Gotzkowsky had done this. What he was, he had become by his own unaided efforts ; not by patronage, nor hypocrisy, nor flattery, not through treachery and subserviency, only by the power and energy of his mind, had he subdued and ruled the envy and jealousy of the world.

As he was now forced to have recourse to its assistance and commiseration, the world naturally attacked him, rending him with its poisonous teeth, rejoicing in his misery, and viewing with satisfaction the humiliation of the once proud and wealthy merchant.

Gotzkowsky arrived at the Town Hall and

slowly ascended the staircase. How often had he done so before, to obey the pressing appeal for help which the magistrates had made to him! how often had he, in this very hall, counselled the counsellors, and lent them his talent and his energy, his credit and his gold!

To day the doors did not fly open before him; the porter at the gate was no longer obsequious, but came forward without any greeting, desiring him to wait in the ante-room till he inquired whether the assembled magistrates wished him to be admitted.

Gotzkowsky waited a considerable time; at last the door opened and he was ushered in.

There sat the senators and councillors, with their worthy burgomaster, just as they had done when they had sought refuge from imminent peril in Gotzkowsky's aid and counsel—the same as when in solemn assembly they decreed him a silver laurel wreath as a token of their gratitude.

Herr von Kircheisen alone was wanting. He was at home delighting his eyes by the sight of Gotzkowsky's gold.

The magistrates on this occasion no longer received him as an adviser and friend, but rather as a kind of delinquent. No one rose to greet him, no one even offered him a seat. They all well knew that he had come to ask something in his turn. Why therefore should they trouble themselves to be polite? He was only a poor petitioner, like a great many other small people.

Gotzkowsky, however, did not seem to observe this change of conduct on the part of the magistrates; there was a smile on his lips, and with a proud step he advanced to a chair, and calmly seated himself in it.

A pause ensued, and the burgomaster asked in a cross, sulky tone, "What Gotzkowsky wanted?"

He drew forth a bundle of papers and placed them on the table, saying, "I have brought my accounts."

A panic of terror was visible on the features of the worthy magistrates, and they sat immovable on their chairs, as if turned to stone.

"You seem, respected gentlemen, to have forgotten my just demands," said Gotzkowsky, coolly. "This is not, indeed, surprising; my accounts are rather ancient; four years have elapsed since I had the honour of making the magistrates of Berlin my debtors. I undertook, for their sakes, three separate and dangerous journeys to Königsberg and Warsaw, to negotiate, in the name of Berlin, the amount of the war contribution. I was obliged at that time also, by the orders and in the interest of the magistrates, to take with me some very valuable presents and precious stones. At this moment I will only refer to a stick mounted with brilliants for General Fermore, a snuff box ornamented with a portrait of the Empress, set with fine diamonds, which I presented to Field Marshal Butterlin, from the city of Berlin."*

The members of the magistracy made no answer. They clutched the papers eagerly, examining hastily the different items with sulky discontented faces.

* Gotzkowsky's Life.

Another pause ensued. Nothing was heard but the rustling of the papers, and the low muttering of those who were reckoning up and comparing together the long rows of figures.

Gotzkowsky impatiently rose and went to the window, and, as he looked up to Heaven, his countenance betrayed the anguish and wounded feeling which crushed his heart at this moment. How gladly would he have snatched the papers from these shabby, haggling men, and thrown them in their faces, in all the force of his scorn and indignation! But he thought of his daughter and the honour of his own good name. He was forced to endure it patiently and with due humility.

At last the burgomaster laid down the accounts, and turned his gloomy looks on Gotzkowsky, who had returned to the table with a forced smile on his face, and inwardly vowing to be composed and patient.

"Have you examined my claims, gentlemen?" said he.

"We have read them," answered the burgomaster, in a hard tone; "but the magistrates cannot admit that they are in your debt!"

"No!" cried Gotzkowsky; and, urged on by his bitter feelings, he continued, "I can easily believe it. The authorities seldom know what they owe to others, but vastly well what others owe to them."

"Not at all," said one of the magistrates, with dignity; "we are well aware that we owe you many thanks for the services rendered to the city."

Gotzkowsky burst into a loud, scornful laugh. "Do you really still remember that?" asked he; "I am happy to hear that you have not forgotten that likewise."

"It is true," said the Stadt Rath, in a tone of much unction, "you undertook the affairs of our city by desire of the council, and you also went to see the Empress at Petersburg by our wish, and twice to Warsaw to visit General Fermore, and twice to Saxony to visit our King. We do not deny it. You see the magistrates are perfectly aware of all you have done for them."

"And we are quite prepared to be grateful," said another, "and to serve you so far as lies in our power; but it is quite impossible to acknowledge the correctness of these accounts."

Gotzkowsky looked at him with alarm, and a deep flush mounted to his cheeks. "You refuse to pay?" said he, faintly.

"It grieves us deeply, but we cannot possibly do so."

"You must make an immense deduction from your claim if you expect it ever to be paid," said the burgomaster, in an irritated tone.

"You really dare to propose such a thing to me?" cried Gotzkowsky, burning with rage and shame. "Is it thus you presume to insult the man to whom, on this very spot, four years ago, you vowed eternal gratitude? At that time I sacrificed, for your sake, the repose of my days, the sleep of my nights; for when danger threatened this city there were no magistrates capable of acting; you were all miserable cowards, and clung to me begging for my support. With tears you besought me to save you, and I left my home, my family, my manufactories, for the sole purpose of serving you. At the risk of my life, in the depths of a severe winter, I undertook these journeys—you cared not whether Russian bayonets waylaid and murdered me, or that my health and my life were in daily peril! You thought but of yourselves! I have not put down in my demand the sleepless nights, the troubles and cares, the privations and hardships, the narrow escapes of my very life, which I suffered. I do not ask any reward for my services, I only demand the actual money which I laid out on your affairs, and you have actually the audacity to refuse this?"

"Not at all," said the burgomaster," quite unmoved by Gotzkowsky's noble excitement, "we do not refuse all payment, we only beg you to reduce the amount of the sum."

"You venture to bargain and haggle with me!" cried Gotzkowsky, sternly; "you seem to consider me a retail dealer, who measures out his life and services by the yard, and you wish to pay me by the yard! I leave such miserable chaffering to petty souls like yours! I will never deduct one item from my just claim!"

The burgomaster rose angrily and said, "Do you dare, sir, to insult the noble body of magistrates?"

"No! the magistrates of Berlin insult themselves by their own deeds—they presume to bargain with me!"

"And they have a perfect right to do so," cried the burgomaster, in a shrill and furious voice; "what business had you to play the grand seigneur in our names?"

"Be silent!" cried Gotzkowsky, in such an imperious tone, that the burgomaster started with alarm, and sunk back in his chair.

Gotzkowsky said not a word more. He took his papers from the table, and, casting a look of bitter scorn and anger at the worthy conclave, he tore them up, and threw the fragments at their feet. "I am paid," said he, and with a proud air crossed the room to leave it.

One of the magistrates hurried after him, and held him back.

"You are too hasty," said he; "we shall agree soon, no doubt."

"No!" said Gotzkowsky, striving to extricate himself from his hold, "I do not bargain and argue for my own just rights."

The other still kept fast hold of him. "But, I assure you, we have no wish to decline all payment. If you would only ——"

"Reduce my claim to meet your views?" interrupted Gotzkowsky. "Never! Let me go. All is at an end between us now and for ever!"

"You shall repent having so rudely thrust aside a magistrate," said the burgomaster, in great wrath.

Gotzkowsky turned and measured him with a look of supreme contempt. "I can never repent of having boldly maintained my own honour," said he, proudly; and, without vouchsafing another word or sign to these wise and noble gentlemen, he left the hall and again passed down the street.

## THE JEWS OF THE MINT.

Herr Itzig was a very pious and believing Jew. He kept the Sabbath in the ancient mode; he was charitable to the poor; and allowed no Jewish beggar to leave his door unrelieved.

He was in his room occupied in his morning prayer, and so entirely absorbed in his pious occupation, that he did not hear repeated knocking at his door; but at this moment he heard behind him a calm low voice, saying, "Good morning, Herr Itzig!"

Herr Itzig first murmured through the conclusion of his prayer at a pretty fast pace. Not for all the world would he have delayed finishing every word of it. "Be merciful to us, oh! Jehovah! and help us in our need," muttered he; "and make us pitiful and compassionate to all those who require our aid, as we wish that thou mayest be towards us."

The pious Jew now closed his prayer book and turned slowly round.

The pale, depressed looking man who greeted him with a mournful smile,—was it really he? Was it, indeed, Johann Gotzkowsky, the renowned banker,—the brilliant, idolised hero of the Exchange,—the millionaire before whom all Europe bent?

An expression of malicious pleasure beamed on Itzig's face, but he quickly suppressed it, for the last words of his prayer were still hovering on his lips, and in some degree hallowed them.

"Ah!" said he, in a friendly tone, while stretching out both hands to Gotzkowsky, "the great and all powerful Gotzkowsky does me the favour to visit me. What an honour for my humble abode!"

Gotzkowsky was not taken in by this amiable politeness. He looked at him with an earnest and searching glance, and, drawing a long breath, said, "Listen to me, Itzig. Let us for once he candid. You have probably heard the reports circulated in the city and on the Exchange about me?"

"I have heard them, but I do not believe them," cried Itzig, with a quick change of expression, now looking very grave. "Such reports have certainly reached my ears, but I know well their worth. It is a speculation of Ephraim that your bills may fall in value, and that he may buy them cheap. I know that you are a rich man, and a rich man has always talent; and a man who has talent is cautious, and risks very little, and never becomes security even for his best friend."

"Then I fear I have less talent than you gave me credit for," said Gotzkowsky; "I have often pledged my name for others."

"Then, of course, you are prepared to pay?" said Itzig, with a forced smile.

"But if it be not in my power to pay?" said Gotzkowsky, sorrowfully.

Itzig stepped back and stared at him in horror.

"If at this moment, at least, I cannot pay," repeated Gotzkowsky, in an urgent voice;

"what if I were unable to pay one half-million for Leipzig, another half-million for the Russian subsidy, after having lost yesterday, by the new law about the light coinage, almost a similar sum? What would you say then, Itzig?"

Itzig had listened to him with increasing terror, and his features had by degrees assumed an aspect of rage and hatred. When Gotzkowsky ceased speaking, he raised his clasped hands to Heaven, as if wishing to call down its judgments on the criminal's head. "God of my fathers!" exclaimed he; "you will then become bankrupt!"

Gotzkowsky seized his hand, and looked at his quivering face with deep and imploring anxiety.

"Hear me, Itzig! I may yet be saved. All depends on my obtaining some delay, that my credit may remain entire. You are rich——"

"No, no! poor—very poor!" interrupted Itzig, eagerly; "quite a poor man! I have nothing but what I earned myself."

"But you have earned a good deal," said

Gotzkowsky, with a faint smile. "Make me a loan, and take my word as security."

"Your word!" cried Itzig, shaking off his hand. "What good would your word be to me? I could not borrow on it."

"Oh! think that the honour of my name is at stake, which I have hitherto preserved pure before God and man!" cried Gotzkowsky, impetuously.

"And if my own good name were at stake," screamed Itzig, "I would rather give it up than my money. Money makes me a man. I am a Jew. I have nothing but money,—it is my life and my honour,—I cannot part with it."

Gotzkowsky would not allow himself to be so easily repulsed. He felt as if his future fate—his existence—his good name—all hung on this moment, like the gambler who places his last stake on one desperate throw. If this failed, there was no more hope for him—no more happiness on earth—nothing save a grave.

With passionate impetuosity Gotzkowsky again seized the hand of the wealthy Jew banker.

"Oh!" said he, imploringly, "remember

that hour of need when you vowed eternal gratitude to me."

"I would never have made that vow," said Itzig, sulkily, "never, by the God of my fathers! if I had for a moment believed that you would ever stand in need of my gratitude."

"My honour must be saved!" cried Gotzkowsky, with heart-rending earnestness. "Do you not understand that my good name is dearer to me than life itself? Remember your oath. Let your heart beat with kindness and sympathy,—be for once a man towards a fellow-man. Make me a loan on my word of honour, —nay, not on that alone,—take my house and all I have for further security. Lend me the sum I require,—I will one day repay it with royal magnificence. Assist me in this great strait, and my gratitude towards you shall be boundless. You have a heart,—have compassion on me!"

Itzig looked at his pale quivering features with a spiteful smile.

"So!" said he, "does the great wealthy Christian banker really admit, in his hour of extremity, that the poor despised Jew has a heart? Well! I have a heart; but I should like to know what that has to do with money? Where business begins, a heart ends. No; I have no heart to lend you money."

Gotzkowsky did not answer immediately,—he stood stunned and motionless. His soul was bruised, and he scarcely felt conscious of the extent of the stroke. He only thought and knew that he was a ruined man, and that the lofty edifice of his fortune was fast crumbling away to bury him in its ruins. He clasped his hands together, and, looking up to Heaven with anguish, he murmured, in a low voice, "Thou seest my misery, oh God! I have done all I could; I have humbled myself to the most urgent entreaties—to the most degraded supplications. Will no providential hand now appear to me out of the cloud?"

"You should have prayed sooner," said Itzig, with cruel mockery. "You should have asked for a little more foresight and judgment."

Gotzkowsky heeded him not. He was struggling manfully with his burden of misery, and, as he was a man of strong mind, and accustomed to self command, at last he conquered himself. He had been for one short interval faint hearted and desperate; but now he was restored to all the strength of his energetic nature.

He raised his drooping head, and his features were resolute and determined. "Well," said he, calmly, "I have left no means untried, —now I accept my fate with resignation. Hear me, Herr Itzig; I must proclaim myself bankrupt,—my house must fall!"

Itzig, suddenly seized by fresh terror, started back. "Heavens!" cried he, "I bought one of your bills only yesterday; surely you will pay that one now?"

"I will not do it, because I cannot," said Gotzkowsky; "and, even if I could, I would not. I have humbled myself before you, and crawled in the dust at your feet, and you have extended no friendly hand to save me. Farewell! and may the worst now come, which you could have prevented, but would not. You will bring a just punishment on yourself. Farewell!"

Itzig clutched his coat frantically, and exclaimed in a voice choked with rage, "Pay me the bill I hold of yours!"

"I will not," said Gotzkowsky, exasperated; "you have decided,—so take your righteous reward."

He pushed past him, and hastily quitted the house; but as he went he heard the loud groans and lamentations of Itzig, imploring Heaven and Hell to punish the criminal who wished to cheat him of his money.

## THE LEIPZIG MERCHANTS.

WEARY and exhausted, Gotzkowsky returned to his house, and, shutting himself up in his own rooms, he yielded entirely to the mournful and dreadful thoughts which tortured him.

He could not conceal the sad truth from himself. The sword was suspended over his head only by two slender hairs. If De Neufville did not return from Amsterdam, and if the courier from Leipzig brought no aid, he was irretrievably ruined, and the sword must infallibly fall.

For the first time he thought of death, and the thought made him almost happy and cheerful. He could always die. He was not obliged to bear the tortures and humiliations of this life. He could seek a sure refuge in the still and silent grave, under clods of earth, which would for ever stifle his groans and cries of anguish, and soon cover his unhappy remains with flowers. He had laboured so hard, his feet were weary, his breast oppressed by the anxieties of this passing world. Why should he not lie down in the grave to rest?—there to dream, or rather to sink for ever into the arms of everlasting sleep,—to wake only in eternity. But he thrust aside these tempting thoughts; he had not yet given up all hope, and his sanguine nature was animated afresh, when at this moment the door opened, and the servant gave him a large sealed letter, which the courier, who had this moment returned, had brought from Leipzig.

With a hasty hand he seized it, and made a sign to Peter to leave the room; but when he was once more alone, and on the point of breaking the seal, he shuddered and paused. This letter might, indeed, bring him safety, or it might bring him his death warrant. He gazed at it with a look of anguish, and weighing it in his hand, muttered, "It is as light as a feather, and yet so weighty that its contents may cast me into an abyss."

"This is weak and foolish," said he, aloud; "I will at least ascertain my fate, and see clearly into futurity."

He broke the seal with a firm hand.

While reading it, horror and dismay were visible on his countenance; his whole frame quivered, and he threw the paper violently on the floor, and said with deep emotion, "This, this is my reward!—reproaches, accusations, instead of thanks,—insult and malice instead of sympathy or aid; reproaches that I ever served them; accusations that I only affected to intercede in their favour, because without me the King of Prussia would never have succeeded in obtaining so large a sum of money from the City of Leipzig. Had I not interfered, they say, they would never have paid at all; but would only have endured a little longer the miseries of imprisonment, which would have been far easier to bear than the loss of such enormous sums.*

He paced the room in much agitation, and,

* Biography of a Patriotic Merchant.

when he passed the letter on the floor, he pushed it aside with his foot, like a venomous snake, which no one would touch.

"I have deserved this punishment!" said he, after a long pause. "Why did I show love for my fellow creatures? why did I assist them in their extremity, instead of falling on them like a highwayman and plundering them when unable to defend themselves?—fool that I was!"

He threw himself into a chair and fell into deep thought. Once more he reviewed his past life; and, while summing up all the events of his existence, he could not but feel that the sum of his happy hours had been small, and his failing and heavy-burdened years great enough now to crush him to the earth.

There was still one hope to cling to. So long as De Neufville's return was expected all was not utterly lost; he must endeavour to struggle against his feeling of desperation, and endure the worst with patience and resolution. He was absorbed in these heart-rending reflections, when the door opened, and Elise entered, her face beaming with joy. She was so intensely happy that, in the agitation of her delight, she did not observe how gloomy and careworn her father looked.

"Oh!" said she, tenderly kissing his hand, "how glad I am to find you at home at last; I have sought you here several times."

"To give me letters?" asked he, hastily; for he had scarcely looked in Elise's face, and had not remarked her joyous air.

Both were too much occupied with their own thoughts and feelings to think of or to observe each other particularly.

"You have letters for me, my child?" repeated Gotzkowsky, anxiously.

"No," said she, with a bright smile. "No letters, but much happiness."

"So De Neufville himself is arrived at last," cried her father, starting up in great excitement, and hurrying to the door.

Elise held him back, and asked in surprise, "What of De Neufville?"

Gotzkowsky gazed at her face, so brightly lit up by her recent happiness, and smiled mournfully.

"Poor fool!" murmured he, in a low tone; "I complain of the egotism of mankind, and am myself egotistical enough to think only of my own anxieties in the presence of my child."

He embraced Elise with a look of inexpressible love and tenderness, and said, "Well, my own darling! tell me what is the happiness you promise me?"

"Look at me," said she, playfully; "can you not read it in my face?"

He gazed sadly into her large sparkling eyes.

"Oh!" said he, fondly, "your eyes shine like two bright hopeful stars; they are the last which will ever shine for me."

Elise threw her arms round his neck and kissed him, and then gently drew him down on a couch, placing herself at his feet on a footstool.

"How often," said she, "how often, father, have you sat here occupied with care for me! Ah! I know well how much sorrow I have caused you during the last four years; I could not command my heart to forget. You knew that, and were ever as gentle and considerate as a mother could have been—the best of fathers! You never reproached or blamed me for my sadness; you saw it, and you did not deny me the luxury of tears."

She kissed his hand, and leant her glowing face on it: after a few moments she said, "See! I weep no longer, or, if I do, they are tears of joy. Father, I am here to implore your blessing—Féodor is arrived; he comes to ask you to bestow me on him as his wife. Oh! forgive him, and consecrate with your blessing our love, which has hitherto been the greatest misery of my life, but will now form its sole happiness."

She laid her head on her father's breast in blushing agitation and shyness.

Gotzkowsky was stunned by the sudden shock; his face became even more pallid and sorrowful than before. He pressed his child's head fondly to his breast, and, while looking upwards with tears in his eyes, he murmured with anguish, "This, too! Oh, God! I am severely tried. This is the most severe sacrifice of all; but my pride is crushed. I bring thee this offering also."

"Father, dear father, you do not answer me," asked Elise, still resting her head on his breast; "you will not refuse your consent and blessing; you will forgive Féodor the follies and short-comings of his early youth, and accept him as your son?"

Gotzkowsky's eyes were still turned upwards, and his lips moved in silent prayer; at last, after a long and distressing conflict with himself, he said solemnly, "Let it be so, I give my consent."

Elise uttered a cry of joy and kissed him fondly, amid tears of the most unalloyed happiness, and, though often interrupted by her agitation, she told him of her interview with Féodor, Lodoiska's death, and her letter."

"How happy would I be at this hour," said she, after finishing her narrative, "how truly happy, if I could only remain with you. Love calls on me to leave you, and yet it also holds me back to stay. I promised Féodor to go with him, but I did it in haste, because I saw only him, and listened only to his entreaties. Now, I see you, dearest father, and it seems to me as if I could not leave you this very day."

"To-day!" cried Gotzkowsky, and a flash of joy lit up his face. His soul was filled with gratitude to God, to whom he had so earnestly prayed in the depth of his grief. Was it not a sign that God was with him still, though men had deserted him? that God had compassion on him, when all had steeled their hearts against him?

This very day his child was to leave him to fulfil a brilliant destiny. He had no further occasion therefore to be anxious about his daughter's fate, and, as she was to set off for Russia with her lover the same night, he was thus spared the torture of being obliged to confess to her his disgrace and his humiliation. He once more kissed Elise tenderly, and said, with a passionate impulse he could not resist, "Farewell, my child, my own and only darling, my sole happiness! You must leave me,—I shall be alone,—but I shall have time to think of you and to pray for you."

He almost pushed her from him, for he felt that his grief would quickly overpower his self command. "Go," said he hurriedly, "go, your husband expects you! You must assume your bridal attire."

Elise smiled. "Yes, I will adorn myself," said she, "but, dear father, you will yourself place the bridal wreath on my hair. That is the last pious office of love with which a mother yields up her daughter to another. I have no mother. You have been both father and mother to me. You will place the myrtle garland on my head?"

"Yes," said he sighing, "I will do so; God grant that it may never become a crown of thorns! Now go, my child, adorn yourself, and leave me alone to pray for you." He smiled on her fondly and led her to the door.

When she had left the room, he felt keenly the sad solitude to which his life was hereafter condemned, and, pressing his hands to his heart to suppress the cry which he would fain have uttered, he said in a low voice, "I have lost her for ever! she is no longer mine! all is torn from me at once! The unfortunate are always alone."

The servant at this moment entered and announced Herr Ephraim. A flash of joyful surprise flew to Gotzkowsky's face, and, while hastily advancing towards the rich Jew, he thought, "Is it possible that this man is come to take pity on my unhappy position? is he more magnanimous than Itzig, and intends to grant me his aid?"

---

## EPHRAIM THE TEMPTER.

"You have come to me?" asked Gotzkowsky eagerly, as Ephraim entered and greeted him in silence. Gotzkowsky's quick eye, however, soon detected in Ephraim's scornful, wrinkled face that it was by no means compassion or sympathy which had brought the Jew to him, but that he had probably come only to feast on the agonies of his victim. "He shall not enjoy that triumph," thought Gotzkowsky; "he shall find me calm and resolute, and never guess all I really suffer."

He forced a cheerful expression into his features, and, while placing a chair for the silent Ephraim, he said, smiling, "Truly, I must be in desperate straits when birds of prey already hover near me! Do you even now scent my death, Herr Ephraim? By heavens, you would enjoy it?"

"You are angry with me," said Ephraim,

slowly shaking his head; "but you shall discover how unjust you are. I bring you an important and a dreadful piece of news."

"It must indeed be dreadful," interrupted Gotzkowsky, "when you grant yourself the great pleasure of announcing it to me."

Ephraim shrugged his shoulders, and said abruptly, "De Neufville is bankrupt!"

A cry of horror escaped Gotzkowsky's lips; he staggered back, and was obliged to support himself on a chair, not to sink to the ground. This was the last deadly stroke, and it had wounded him to death

"De Neufville has failed?" murmured he, hoarsely.

"Yes, he is bankrupt!" said Ephraim, with ill-concealed joy. "The proud Christian merchant who delighted in looking down with lofty contempt on the poor Jew, Ephraim, is now a bankrupt. The Jew of the Mint is prosperous and afloat still—the Christian merchant has stopped payment, and is ruined for ever!"

While he so spoke, he broke into a wild and scornful laugh, which immediately restored Gotzkowsky to his usual calmness and self-possession.

"You are triumphant," said he, "and your malicious pleasure at my ruin is visible in your face. You have conquered, for De Neufville's failure is your work. It was you who so long persecuted him, and undermined his credit by your insinuations and calumnies, till you succeeded in shaking it, and the whole edifice of his honest labours crumbled to the ground."

"It is my work!" said Ephraim, with spiteful pleasure. "He stood in my way, and I have shoved him aside. What more have I done! Life is a battle—he who has most strength, that is, most gold, remains the conqueror."

"De Neufville failed! this is indeed a hard blow," whispered Gotzkowsky; and, as his wandering glance met the watchful eyes of the Jew, he said, in a tone of entire exhaustion,

"Revel in my misery if you like—you have succeeded—you have stabbed me to the heart."

"Listen to me, Gotzkowsky," said Ephraim, "I wish you well."

"Oh! yes," cried Gotzkowsky, bitterly, "after you have hastened my ruin, you make a pretence of loving me!—but I ought to believe in your friendship, for no one but a friend could have had the heart to bring me such bad news."

Ephraim shook his head slightly. "Hear me!" said he, "I will be perfectly candid with you. I hated you formerly because you were more powerful and more wealthy than myself. You were highly esteemed. Your uprightness, your honour, your punctuality were proverbial—that vexed my pride. When an important affair was to be concluded, there was no confidence in its success unless Gotzkowsky undertook it; and when your signature was appended to any contract every one was satisfied—your name was as good as money—that provoked me."

"And for this base envy and jealousy you wished to ruin me!" exclaimed Gotzkowsky. "On this account you have incessantly laboured to ensure my destruction! Because you knew that I expected this supply of light gold from Hamburg, you——"

"Succeeded in having this deficient coin

pronounced illegal. It is true; it was all owing to my exertions. From this day forth I am both richer and more influential than you; but you shall see that I only hate your firm, and not yourself. I come to assist you. You must, indeed, become bankrupt—that is inevitable, not all the efforts you can possibly make can save you from this stroke—you must and will stop payment, and this very day, too."

Gotzkowsky muttered some confused words, and covered his face with his hands. "It is, alas, too true!" said he, in bitter grief. "I have at last made shipwreck with all my hopes."

Ephraim laid his hand hastily on Gotzkowsky's shoulder. "Then endeavour, at least, to save a plank from the wreck on which you can swim safely to shore," whispered he. "You can no longer save your creditors,—at least save yourself."

Gotzkowsky removed his hands from his face, and looked in utter surprise at Ephraim, who met his look of inquiry with a smiling mysterious aspect, and, coming close to him, whispered in his ear: "I mean that you must not be such a fool as to give up all you have to your creditors, and to quit this house an actual pauper. Save yourself. Entrust your most important papers to me, and all that you possess in money or money's worth. I will carefully secrete it. You are silent? Be reasonable, my good sir. Do not give the world the pleasure of pitying you. The world does not deserve so agreeable a pastime. Believe me, men are very bad, and he is no Solomon who wishes to be better than all the others."

He was silent, and looked searchingly at Gotzkowsky, who returned his glance with one of supreme contempt.

"So this is your love!" said he. "You would make me a swindler."

"Every man swindles his neighbour," said Ephraim, coolly; "why should you alone be honest?"

"Because I do not choose to be ashamed of myself. It is the fault of others if I stop payment to-day; but no one shall ever say that Gotzkowsky has burdened his own soul with guilt."

"They will say it all the same," interposed Ephraim. "He who is unfortunate is always guilty in the eyes of his fellow men. And do you think, that, if he could serve himself at the expense of others, and did not,—do you believe he will be the more esteemed on that account? No, believe me, he will only be laughed at and ridiculed. I have often lamented over you, Gotzkowsky, for, with all your cleverness, your life has been only one long mistake."

"Or rather say," answered the other, impatiently, "that I have never profited by my experience of the knavery of others."

"You have been sadly in error," continued the Jew, "for you have calculated on gratitude. That capital is badly laid out which brings in no interest. If a man is grateful he must be ruined, for those around him never are. He who would succeed in the world must above all think only of himself and his own advantage."

"There you are right, sage of this world!" said Gotzkowsky, with a bitter laugh.

"If I had thought like you," continued Ephraim, quite unmoved, "I could not possibly have striven to ruin you, nor could I have procured the change in the law of coinage. In that case, indeed, I should have been grateful, but I should have done no business. Now, I first secured my profit, and after that I came here to serve you, and to show you my gratitude."

"I wish for no gratitude. Let me go my path and you go yours."

Ephraim looked at him with almost sincere compassion.

"Leave me," cried Gotzkowsky. "You shall not deprive me of my last possession,—a good conscience."

"A good conscience!" said the Jew, with a sneering laugh. "I think a man might soon starve on such a capital as that."

At this moment there were heard outside loud shouts and cheers, and the sound of military music.

King Frederick the Second was returning this day to Berlin, after a long absence, and the happy joyful citizens had prepared a solemn and brilliant procession to welcome him. They had unclosed their great gates, and the state carriages, with their emblems, had been all drawn forth to bring the King into his gaily decorated city. The procession must pass Gotzkowsky's house, and the sounds of gay music were heard gradually approaching, and the cries and shouts of the people sounded ever louder and louder.

Ephraim opened the window, and pointing down to the street, he said, with a spiteful laugh, "Look here, Gotzkowsky! this is a satisfactory proof of your fine, lofty sentiments! How often has Berlin called you her benefactor, and yet it is making merry on the very day which seals your ruin! The whole town knows that Gotzkowsky must stop payment to-day, and yet they pass close by your house with gay music and shouts, and not one person thinks of you."

"He is right," said Gotzkowsky, as the cries were heard close under his windows, "he is right—I was a fool to love my fellow creatures."

Ephraim again resumed: "See," said he, "here comes Count Salen, whom you, when the Russians were here, saved from death. He does not look up! Ah! there goes the banker Splittgerber, whose manufactories in Neustadt-Eherswald you at that time preserved for him. He does not look up either! Yes, he does, he looks up and laughs! See! now comes the King, with his staff of generals. You have done the King many a good service; you fulfilled his favourite wishes; you erected the first large manufactories here for velvets and silks; you founded the porcelain manufactory; you travelled to Italy at your own expense, to purchase pictures for the King; you saved his capital from being plundered by the Austrians and Russians. The Dutch minister, Von Verelse, who at that same period interceded with the Austrians for Berlin, the King, as a mark of his gratitude, has raised to the rank of Count.* What did he do for you? Verelse's was a trifling service compared with yours. I say again, what did the King do for you? Look! the King and his staff have passed by and not one of them glanced up here! Yesterday they would have done so, for yesterday you were still rich; but to-day they have already forgotten you, for you are now poor, and the memory of men is very defective for *poor* people. Ah! you may look down, Gotzkowsky; there are a great many people hurrying past, many noble gentlemen, too, whom you have obliged—but not one glances your way!"

Gotzkowsky had almost involuntarily advanced to the window, and, irritated by Ephraim's words, he looked down on the brilliant procession passing under his windows with an anxious, dreary longing. What would he not have given that one, only *one*, of the many who had once called themselves his

* Prussia: Frederick the Great, vol. ii. page 255.

friends, would look up and greet him with kindly sympathy! But Ephraim was right—no one thought of him who was leaning on the window with a broken heart, no longer hoping for assistance, but only for a little love, a little sympathy.

Suddenly Gotzkowsky's face brightened, and he pointed to the procession. "You are right, Ephraim," said he, "the noble and the distinguished do not look up here—but here comes the close of the procession; here come the poor, the lowly, the honest workpeople. See how they look at me, and greet me, and wave their caps. Ah! there is one man pressing his hand to his eyes. He is a poor fellow who worked formerly in my manufactory. The man is weeping because he knows that I am unhappy. There come others—poor people in ragged clothes, women with babies in their arms, infirm old men—they all look up at me, do you see? they smile, and the children extend their little hands towards me. Ah! these poor people still love me, though I am no longer rich!" And, turning to Ephraim, with eyes dimmed by tears of sweet emotion, he said, "I have not miscalculated—no! you are mistaken—I counted on the kernel, and not on the hard shell. I have reposed my trust in the people, and my confidence has not been misplaced."

Ephraim shrugged his shoulders. "The people are very capricious," said he, "they will stone to-morrow the man they idolize to-day; wait till you are condemned by public opinion—see how the people will treat you then! Take my advice, collect your papers and valuables and entrust them to me. I swear to you to keep them for you faithfully."

"Away, tempter!" cried Gotzkowsky indignantly; "I am resolved that, in spite of my misfortunes, there shall be written on my tombstone, 'He died poor, but honest.'"

"Fool, fool!" exclaimed Ephraim with a sneer, "you are speculating on your epitaph and rejecting the goods of this world; think of your daughter, if not of yourself."

"What gives you a right to remind me of her?" said Gotzkowsky indignantly; "do not desecrate her name by alluding to her. Go, I have not one feeling in common with you."

"Yes, you have," said Ephraim, "you once benefited me, and I was grateful,—that is one feeling in common. I gave you a fine brilliant."

Gotzkowsky did not answer, but crossed the room to his writing table, and took out of a drawer a red morocco case; he opened it, and snatched out the diamond ring it contained."

"I will retain no mark of your gratitude," said he indignantly; "if you could offer me all the treasures of the world, I would cast them at your feet as I do this ring!" and he threw the valuable jewel on the floor beside Ephraim, who coolly picked it up, and looked at him earnestly, then broke into a loud insolent laugh.

"This is the very same ring," said he, "which our community presented to you when you freed us from the hearth tax. You give it to me?"

"I do give it to you, and my curse with it,

tempter of honest men! If your hand could save me from a precipice I would spurn it."

"So be it, then," said Ephraim, his face breathing hatred, malice, and disappointment. It was evident he keenly felt that he, the wealthy Ephraim, had been conquered by Gotzkowsky, though now a poor, ruined, shipwrecked man; and that all attempts to drag him in the mud had failed from Gotzkowsky's stern integrity.

"So be it," repeated Ephraim, "you will have it so! I accept the ring, and I will tell you what use I intend to make of it—I will buy a place with it in the churchyard, that the dishonourable bankrupt may at least find an honourable grave, and not be shovelled into the earth like the suicide De Neufville."

"What do you say? De Neufville dead!" cried Gotzkowsky, going up to Ephraim, who was leaving the room, and seizing his arm eagerly—

"Say it again, is De Neufville really dead?"

Ephraim seemed to enjoy Gotzkowsky's look of anguish, and repeated slowly,

"De Neufville made away with himself because he would not survive his shame!" and with a loud laugh he passed through the door, slamming it violently.

Gotzkowsky stood on the same spot in the deepest grief. He had not only lost in De Neufville a friend whom he loved, and on whose fidelity he could depend, but his own future fate and his last hope were gone down to the grave with him.

"He killed himself; and am I to live?" whispered Gotzkowsky gloomily: "he was right—when shame begins, life should end. An existence without honour, a prolonged life of disgrace and misery! My friend has shown me the way; I will consider of it—but not here; in the privacy of my cabinet, where I shall be alone and undisturbed, where no one will come to interrupt me, I will consider of it there," and with a look of despair he hastened to his cabinet, carefully closing and bolting the door behind him.

## ELISE.

HER bridal attire was completed, and her face beaming with happiness; smiling and weeping by turns, Elise was standing before a large Venetian mirror in her dressing-room, looking at the reflection of her own loveliness. Not from vanity, or to admire either her dress or her beauty, but simply to convince herself that it was no dream, no flight of fancy, or of a lovesick heart, but that it was truth, delightful reality. When she saw in the mirror the reflection of herself in her white dress, with her blushing cheeks, she smiled.

"Is not my dress too simple?" said she; "no ornaments, only plain white silk; the very excess of my love and joy has made me forget all else—I forgot that he comes from the land of diamonds, and that he is a Prince—I will deck myself in a manner worthy of my bridegroom."

She took from her jewel box the valuable set of diamonds, the heritage she had received from her mother, and fastened the sparkling brilliants in her ears and on her arms, and then the superb necklace of alternate emeralds and diamonds on her white throat.

"Now I look like a Princess indeed," said she, looking at herself once more in the mirror. "Perhaps I may please him thus; but the best adornment of all is yet wanting—my bridal wreath; but my father must place it on my head himself."

As she took up her myrtle wreath and gazed at it, she became serious and thoughtful.

"It is the crown of love and of death," whispered she. "When a young girl dies, it is placed on her head if she dies unmarried, to rise again as a purified spirit in the realms of bliss.—I thank thee, oh God! that thou hast permitted me to enjoy happiness here, and my future life shall testify my gratitude."

Feeling oppressed and solitary within the walls of her lonely room, she resolved to go to her father, to throw herself into his arms, and to pour out to him all her love, her happiness, and her tender filial affection and gratitude. She took up the myrtle wreath, and flitted like a gazelle through the corridor which led to her father's apartments.

How her white silk dress rustled, how the brilliants shone and glistened, leaving a train of light like a comet, as she glided along the dusky corridor!

With a happy smile, and her bridal wreath in her hand, she entered her father's room—but it was empty; she crossed it rapidly to seek him in his cabinet—the door was locked, and no one answered either her knock or her call. He must have gone out, and would undoubtedly return immediately.

She sat down to wait for him, and sunk into a happy reverie. What sweet and precious dreams hovered round her—what blissful prospects for the future greeted her!

The door opened, and Elise started up to meet her father—it was only Bertram; and how changed he was, how pale, how sad! He scarcely looked at her; his eye passed over her without seeing her. What was it which had changed him so suddenly? Did he already know that Elise was to be married on this very day, and that her long lamented lover was returned?

She asked him eagerly if he had seen her father.

"Good God! is he not here?" cried Bertram, starting violently. "I must speak to him instantly, for I have a most important communication to make to him, which does not admit of a moment's delay."

Elise looked at him in surprise. She had never seen him so excited; every fibre of his frame seemed to be on the stretch; and involuntarily she trembled as she asked him the cause of his agitation and anxiety.

Bertram denied being agitated, and yet he continued to look round eagerly, and was evidently a prey to considerable uneasiness and alarm.

This made Elise still more desirous to know the source of his unusual excitement. She urged him again to tell her its cause, but Bertram once more declared that nothing was wrong.

Elise shook her head sorrowfully. "I am not so easily deceived," said she; "I see misfortune written in your face;" and, suddenly penetrated with an unaccountable presentiment of terror, she added, turning pale, "You are bringing bad news to my father."

Bertram did not answer, but, unable to stand her searching glance, he cast down his eyes.

Anxiety and alarm suddenly awoke within the tender daughter's heart, and she trembled while entreating him eagerly to say what misfortune threatened her father.

Bertram could no longer resist telling her the truth.

"She must know it, sooner or later," thought he; "it is better that she should hear it from me than from a stranger."

He took her hand, and leading her to a sofa, and seating himself beside her, he related to her slowly and cautiously, endeavouring as much as possible to spare her feelings, the losses and misfortunes which had befallen her father.

Elise had little experience of the practical misfortunes of life. She, who had never known even a moment's privation, could not in the least comprehend that happiness or honour were in any degree linked with money. When Bertram ended she breathed heavily, as if wishing to relieve her full heart.

"How you terrified me!" said she smiling. "So this is all the misfortune? we shall be poor? My father cares not for wealth."

"But for honour!" said Bertram.

"Oh, my father's honour can never be in danger," cried Elise proudly.

Bertram shook his head sorrowfully.

"It is in danger at this very moment," said he. "We have the certain conviction of his innocence, but the world will not believe in it. They will forget all his noble deeds, his magnanimity and generosity; they will efface all memory of the past, and only remember that to-day, for the first time in his life, he cannot redeem his pledged word. They will condemn him, and affix to his hitherto honoured name, in common with the basest deceivers, the epithet of bankrupt."

Elise looked at him while he was speaking with increasing alarm. She felt for the first time the whole weight of the misfortune which impended over her father, and shuddered as she realised the dreadful truth. Wringing her hands, and her eyes dimmed with tears, she asked Bertram eagerly if there really was no hope of rescuing her father from this fearful calamity.

"His credit is undermined," said Bertram with a sigh; "I know no one in this world who can extricate him."

"No one?" asked Elise, placing her hand kindly on his shoulder; "and you, my brother?"

"Alas! I have done all that was in my power," said he; and, even at this moment of anxiety, her touch seemed to electrify him.

"I have implored him with tears in my eyes to accept the little I possess; to grant me the sacred rights of a son; but he refused absolutely to comply with my wish. He will not hear of one unconnected with him sacrificing himself. I know that my whole property cannot save him, but it might perhaps delay the moment of his fall, or at least assist in covering the amount of his debts; but he is inexorable. He repeats that, if I were really his son, he would accept my offer at once. Elise," continued he, forgetting in the pressing extremity all fear, "I did not even hesitate in this moment of desperation to entreat him to give me your hand. I know you do not love me, but you could have esteemed me for the love I bear your father. If he had permitted you to make this sacrifice to filial affection, you would have accepted my hand to save your father from destruction?"

He was silent, and looked timidly at the young girl, trembling and blushing at his side. She felt that he deserved an answer; and, when she looked up and saw his noble countenance, which had never varied, never changed in love and devotion to her, when she thought of his disinterested affection, which had suffered in silence, only striving for her happiness and peace, she felt the deepest emotion, and, for the first time, a feeling of tender sorrow and sympathy for Bertram. She stretched out her hand to him with a look of sincere gratitude.

"Bertram," said she, "of all men whom I have ever known, you are the most noble. My soul reveres you, and my heart would love you, were it my own to give."

Bertram bent over her hand and kissed it; in doing so, his eye was attracted by the sparkling ornaments she wore, and he now was first aware of her unusually brilliant attire, and asked in surprise the cause.

"Oh, do not think of it now," cried Elise, "speak to me of my father. What did he answer when you asked him for my hand?"

"That he would never accept such a sacrifice from his daughter, even were it to save him from instant death."

"Is his ruin quite inevitable?" asked Elise thoughtfully.

"I almost fear it is," sighed Bertram; "this very morning reports of that nature were circulated in the city; and your father himself told me that, if Russia persisted in her demands, he must be irretrievably lost. Judge, then, of my consternation at receiving from a friend at Petersburg this morning the certain intelligence that the Empress has already despatched a special ambassador to wind up this affair without delay. This half-million must be very precious in the Empress's eyes, for, on account of it, she parts with her well-known favourite and minion Prince Stratimojeff."

Elise started up in alarm, and asked Bertram, "Who does the Empress send?"

"Her lover, Prince Stratimojeff," repeated Bertram calmly.

Elise trembled, her eyes shot fire, and her cheeks glowed.

"What right have you," said she indignantly, "so to insult Prince Stratimojeff as to call him the lover of this dissolute Empress?"

Bertram looked at her in amazement.

"What care you for this Prince?" said he, "all the world knows that he is one of Katherine's minions. Read what my correspondent says."

He took out a letter from his pocket, and showed Elise the passage where a detailed account was given of the mission of the Imperial envoy, who was designated the Empress's lover, and of Orloff's accession to favour.

Elise uttered a faint cry, and sunk back on the sofa.

There was a ringing in her ears, the blood seemed to rush to her heart, suffocating her, and she murmured, in a faltering voice, "I shall die! I shall die!" but this momentary stupefaction passed away, and Elise became conscious of her position. She now understood it all. With self-reproach for her credulity, she recalled her interview with Féodor, and endeavoured to take a calm view of the distressing circumstances in which she was at this moment placed. So this was the cause of the hasty betrothal, and the written consent of the Empress to their marriage! Superseded in Katherine's favour by another, he wished to present a young bride to society, to prove that these reports had been all calumny, that he might say to the world, "This is my young bride, and the Empress Katherine is as pure as an angel!" She was to serve as a cloak for the past. She sprang up, and paced the room in extreme agitation—her whole being was in a state of excitement.

She shuddered at the abyss of misery which she had so narrowly escaped. She thought with horror of the man who not only wished ruthlessly to deceive her, but, in defiance of all feelings of common delicacy, had accepted the office of a hard creditor from his Imperial Mistress, to ensure the ruin of her own father. She heeded not Bertram's astonishment, who in vain sought for an explanation of this strange emotion.

"It is too much!" said she half aloud, "even love cannot submit to such an outrage. Love! away with the word! I would despise myself, if one spark of such a holy feeling were still to linger in my heart for such a traitor. I will show him my abhorrence, and have my revenge. He shall see how heartily I despise him!" cried she aloud; and, like an aroused tigress, she snatched up the myrtle wreath from the table. "The bond of love is broken, and I will annihilate it as I do this bridal wreath!" cried she wildly; but suddenly a gentle hand was placed on hers, and Bertram's mild and sympathising voice met her ear.

What he said, with what words he sought to soothe her, she scarcely knew; but he now understood all the extent of her misfortunes, and words of kindness and consolation flowed from his lips. Though still too benumbed by the shock thoroughly to comprehend his efforts to soften her grief, yet she heard his sympathising voice, and felt she had a friend ready to stretch out his hand to save her from the depths of misery and despair. She would have gone mad, she would have been lost for ever, if the friend of her youth had not stood by her side to inspire her with strength,—she felt it, she knew it. Whenever she was threatened by misfortune, she found him near to guard and watch over her, and to restore her to peace and tranquillity.

"Bertram, Bertram, save me!" said she, trembling in every nerve. "Do not close your heart against me! Have pity on me."

She leant her head on his shoulder and wept bitterly. In the midst of her grief she felt it a real blessing that Bertram was beside her; and, for the first time, a distinct conviction that God had placed him by her side to be her guardian angel, protector, and friend. The delusions and errors of her whole life fell like a veil from before her eyes, and she saw clearly her true relation to Bertram.

When now leaning on him, in the extremity of her sorrow, she thought of all this, her thoughts became prayers, and her tears of regret changed into tears of gratitude.

"I have harboured an angel in my house unawares!" whispered she, involuntarily using the words of Holy Writ; and, when Bertram inquired her meaning, she answered,

"It means that an erring heart has returned at last to the right path."

She hastily dried her tears, scorning to waste another tear on this false, crafty traitor, this degenerate son of a degenerate people. He was not worth a single sigh, not even revenge, no,—not even a reproach!

Elise raised her head and looked at Bertram.

"You asked my father for my hand?" asked she; "do you love me still?"

Bertram smiled, the question seemed to him so strange.

"Love you still?" said he; "could I ever cease to love you?"

"Do you love me still?" repeated she more urgently.

"Faithfully, fondly, and for ever! and that you must know well," said he.

"Faithfully and fondly?" cried Elise deeply moved; "these are words as strong as rocks, and, like the shipwrecked mariner, I will cling fast to them to save myself from destruction. Bertram, how good and unselfish you are! You love my father, and you wish to be his son merely that you may serve him."

"I would gladly work for him, or give my life for him, if necessary."

She looked at him long and searchingly, and stretched out her hand to him.

"Give me your hand, Bertram," said she, in a low voice; "you have been a better son to my father than I have ever been a daughter.

I will henceforth learn from you—will you be my teacher?"

Bertram looked at her in surprise and agitation; she answered his glance with a sweet smile, which shot to his heart with a flash of hope, and made his whole frame quiver.

"Can it be so? is it indeed possible?" murmured he softly; "is my day of suffering drawing to a close? Will——"

Suddenly he was interrupted by Elise starting and seizing his hand. She whispered,

"Silence, Bertram; look there!"

Bertram followed the direction of her eyes, and saw Gotzkowsky, who had opened the door of his cabinet and entered the room. His features were pale and distorted, and his eyes wide open and fixed.

"He does not see us," whispered Elise; "he is talking to himself; do not let us disturb him."

She pointed in silence to a curtain close to them, concealing a recess, in the centre of which was placed a valuable antique vase.

"Let us conceal ourselves," said she; and both, unseen by Gotzkowsky, glided behind the curtain.

## RESCUE.

Gotzkowsky had done with life and earthly things; he had signed the document declaring himself bankrupt, and giving up all his property and possessions of every kind to his creditors. The die was cast—he had become great and powerful through the influence of gold,—now he was no longer great and powerful, for he was poor. Why should he henceforth endure the burden of a life which had lost all illusion for him, and in which his most precious possession, his honour, had been lost? Never again in life would he pass along those streets where once every one had greeted him with reverence and respect, to encounter probably the very men who, regardless of the gratitude they had so often vowed, had, on this very day, chased him away from their doors like an importunate beggar. His corpse alone should pass those men, who had broken his heart. His death should be a monument of their shame, a startling proof of their base ingratitude.

With such thoughts he entered this room, which was to be for him the chamber of death. He was resolved to rid himself of a dishonoured existence, to soar free and unsullied to the regions of light and bliss!

There was in this room a valuable *ètagere,* on which stood the silver goblet the magistrates of Leipzig had presented to him, in token of their gratitude. He was resolved to drink death out of this cup. He took it up, and shook into it a small white powder, which looked so light and harmless, and yet was strong enough to crush him into the grave with iron weight. Then he seized a water-flask, and poured water on the powder—it was prepared, and Gotzkowsky had only to set it to his lips, to drink eternal rest, and eternal forgetfulness of this earth's miseries; but madly to rush with the burden of his sins into eternity!

Elise saw all and understood all. She folded her hands and prayed earnestly; she felt that she must save her father's life or die with him.

"When he lifts the cup I will rush out," whispered she to Bertram, slightly opening the curtain to watch her father.

Gotzkowsky took up the silver wreath of oak leaves, which the city of Berlin had offered to him.

"I deserved it well!" said he, gazing at it with a bitter smile. It was a strange sight to see this lofty, proud figure, these pale, quivering features, and, through an opening in the curtain, the livid, agonised face of his daughter, whose burning eyes were intently fixed on her father.

Gotzkowsky lifted the silver cup,—it almost touched his lips; suddenly he trembled,—a dear and beloved voice uttered his name,—it was the voice of his daughter—whom he had forgotten in the bitterness of his anguish. He had believed that his heart was dead to all feeling, but love still lived within him, and love recalled him to life. It was as if an electric shock had thrilled through his whole being! he set down the cup, and, covering his face with his hands, he murmured,

"Oh! unnatural father, I forgot my child!"

Elise stood behind him, and prayed to God for strength. She wished to appear quite calm and undisturbed, that her father might not suspect she knew of his fatal resolution. Her voice must not falter, her eyes must look bright and clear; she must force a smile to her lips, which still trembled from the fervency of the prayer of anguish she had sent up to her Creator.

"Father!" said she in a low voice but a firm tone, "I come to implore your blessing, and here is the myrtle wreath with which you promised to adorn your child."

Gotzkowsky's face was still hidden; but his whole frame trembled and shook as if from ague.

"I thank thee, Heavenly Father! I thank thee," whispered he; "the voice of my child has saved me from a fearful crime." Suddenly he turned, and, stretching out his arms to her, called out in a loud voice,

"Elise, my child, come to my heart, and console your unhappy father!"

Elise rushed into his arms with a joyful cry, and pressed him close to her heart, whispering words of the most tender sympathy and devoted filial love. They penetrated Gotzkowsky's heart like healing balsam, and forced tears both of joy and remorse into his eyes. He bent his head on Elise's shoulder and wept bitterly.

Long they remained clasped in that fond embrace; their lips were silent, but their hearts mutually spoke, and they understood each other without words. At last Elise extricated herself from her father's encircling arms, and said, with a smile, while offering him the myrtle wreath,

"Now, father, bless your daughter!"

"I will do so," said Gotzkowsky, endeavouring to overcome his emotion; "I will give you my heartfelt blessing; but where is the bridegroom?"

Elise looked at him earnestly.

"Will you welcome him also, father?"

"I will, my child, from my heart I will."

Elise went up to the curtain, and, drawing it aside, she took Bertram by the hand and led him to her father, saying with inimitable grace,

"Father, bless your children!"

"Is this your bridegroom? is it possible?" asked Gotzkowsky joyfully; and, for the first time, a ray of pleasure lit up his wan and worn face.

Bertram had thrown himself at her feet, and seizing her hand, covered it with fond kisses. Elise placed her hand on his shoulder, and said,

"I wish to rest on your heart, Bertram. I will be faithful and true and loving to you, as you have ever been to me. You shall reconcile me with mankind, and restore happiness to my father and myself. We know that, in resting our hopes in you, we shall not do so in vain—is it not so, father?"

She turned to her father and continued,

"Life is still precious, dearest father! it gives you a son who is proud to share your fortunes for good or for evil, and a daughter thankful to be permitted to go through the world with such a father, and to say to all in the depths of our poverty, 'Gotzkowsky is a beggar because he was rich in loving his fellow creatures; he is poor now, because he was so noble hearted himself that he trusted in others!'" and, affectionately embracing him, she said, smiling amid her tears,

"Father, you will no longer think of deserting your children?"

"No, my child, I will live, and live for you!" cried Gotzkowsky, quite overpowered by emotion and joy; "a new existence shall begin for us; we will take refuge in some quiet cottage, far from all the luxury and tinsel for which men strive so hard, and for the sake of which they sacrifice their souls. We shall take none of this world's gewgaws with us,—we give them back to the world. You will not repine, my Elise, at the loss of this vain splendour, if by renouncing it you redeem your father's honour?"

Elise leant her head on his shoulder.

"I was poor," said she, "when all thought me rich; now I am in reality rich, when all the world will call me poor. Give up everything we possess in the world, father; let no one be able to say that Gotzkowsky was in his debt, or that he had broken his pledged word."

She eagerly unfastened the brilliant necklace, earrings, and bracelets, with which she was decorated.

"Take these, too," said she smiling, "add them to the rest; we will retain nothing but our honour and the conviction of a good conscience."

"Now I am your son," cried Bertram with beaming eyes, "I have a right to serve you; you can no longer refuse to accept all I have; we can thus save our house, and satisfy all the creditors."

"We will do so," exclaimed Gotzkowsky. "I accept your noble offer, my son!" and, while joining Elise's hands and Bertram's, he said with deep emotions of thankfulness,

"From this day forth we shall be poor, but yet much richer than many thousands of wealthy men, for we have sound limbs, and strong arms, and willing hearts to labour. We have a good conscience, and that humble yet sure hope, which God grants to those alone who put their trust in Him."

---

## A JUST REWARD.

The appointed hour was arrived, and, adorned in all the splendour of his richly embroidered uniform, covered with orders, glittering with diamonds, which the favour of two empresses had conferred on him, Prince Féodor von Stratimojeff entered Gotzkowsky's house.

He ascended the stair leading to the apartment of his bride with a proud and triumphant aspect. His aim was accomplished at last. This lovely, charming, and wealthy young girl was at length to be his wife! He could present his beautiful bride to the Court of St. Petersburg, and by her attractions, youth, and reputed riches, as well as by his own devotion to Elise, take an ample revenge on the Empress, for her fickleness. These were his thoughts as he gently opened the door, and entered Elise's apartment.

There she stood in her white bridal attire,

delicate, slender, and pure as a lily; her father was also present, and the friend of her youth, Bertram.

They were doubtless to serve as witnesses during the ceremony—there was nothing to be done, but to repair without delay to the altar.

Elise had implored her father that she should herself see and dismiss the Prince, and she had also requested that Bertram should be present. She wished to show him, that by one stroke her heart had been for ever severed from this foolish and ill-regulated passion, and that she could meet Prince Stratimojeff without fear or hesitation. This was a sacrifice she considered due to the honour of her future husband and to her own virgin pride; she would have cordially despised herself, if a single tear or sigh had betrayed the grief which involuntarily oppressed her heart.

She saw, therefore, the Prince enter, and remained cold and composed; and for the first time he no longer appeared to her the same fascinating being she had hitherto considered him; on the contrary, she read in his worn features the melancholy history of his past life. The film which had darkened her eyes was removed. She saw him as he really was—her glance was once more free; and she now shuddered at the wild demoniacal beauty, which she had once idolised as a realisation of all manly perfection. As she looked at him she felt that she could almost hate him, because she had wasted so much fond love on so worthless a being. She had devoted to him her first youth and her first love—he had deprived her of her peace of mind and of the early bloom of her heart; and she had not even the consolation or the right to deplore her lost love; she could only blush for it, and turn away from such once sweet memories with grief and shame.

Féodor approached with an expression of triumph and pride, and, bending low before her father, he said, with a self-satisfied smile, "I come to fetch my bride, and to ask her father to bestow his Elise on me."

He stretched out his hand to Elise, and looked at her with sparkling eyes; but hers remained cold and composed, and her voice did not even tremble.

"Here is a bride," said she, "but not yours, Prince Féodor von Stratimojeff!"

Giving her hand to Bertram, she continued, "This is my husband! He has rescued me from you to-day for the third time!"

Prince Féodor stood aghast, and staggered back.

"Elise, is it thus you reward my love?" asked he, after a pause, reproachfully. "Is this the fidelity which you vowed towards me?"

She came nearer to him, and said in a low voice—

"I preserved a faithful heart for my Féodor, but when he became Prince Stratimojeff he lost it for ever—Elise is too proud to be the wife of the man who is only a Prince because he was the minion of an Empress."

She turned proudly away to leave the room, but Féodor held her back. He had no longer any cause for concealment or reserve—he only felt that he was unutterably miserable, and that every hope of his life had vanished.

"Elise," said he, in the soft and sorrowful tone which had once so fascinated her heart, "I came to you to save me from myself, and you cast me into an abyss! Like a drowning man I stretched out my hand to you—in your love I would have awoke to a new being—but fate is just in ruthlessly hurling me back from this haven of refuge, and I must now be irretrievably lost! Be it so! Let the waves of this life roll over my weary head, but the last cry I utter shall be your dear name!"

Elise listened to him without the slightest emotion,—nay, almost with a smile of contempt.

"You will not find time, amid the pleasures of a court, to think of dying at present," said she, quietly; and, turning to her father, she continued, "My conference with this gentleman is at an end. You can now, father, begin yours."

She gave her hand to Bertram, and, without

vouchsafing another word or look at Féodor, left the room with her betrothed.

"Now, sir," said Gotzkowsky, coldly," let us discuss our affairs. Be so good as to accompany me to my counting-house. You came to Berlin with the intention to rob me of my daughter, and of my money. You have not succeeded in the one,—try if you can succeed better with the other."

"I will indeed,—have no fears of that!" cried the Prince, gnashing his teeth with rage. "Elise has been pitiless to me,—I will be so also to you."

"I would reject your pity with scorn, for I should feel that it only disgraced me," said Gotzkowsky.

"Then we are open enemies to the death!" cried the Prince.

"Not at all," answered Gotzkowsky, coolly; "we are only two individuals bargaining and trafficking together, each endeavouring to gain an advantage. Further than that, we are strangers."

He opened the door, and summoned his two cashiers.

"This gentleman is an agent of Russia," said Gotzkowsky, in a cutting tone. "He has been despatched hither to negotiate with me, and, in case I cannot pay his demands, he is empowered to have recourse to the most severe measures against me. You will, gentlemen, arrange this matter of business with him,—you already have the necessary instructions."

He turned to the Prince, who, breathless and trembling from inward emotion—glowing with rage and sorrow—was leaning against the wall to support himself.

"Prince Stratimojeff," said he, "you shall be paid. Take these thirty thousand dollars, the property of my son-in-law: he joyfully sacrificed this sum to free us from you. Here are further the jewels of my daughter, bequeathed to her by her mother,—take them to the Empress as a worthy memorial of your actions in this country. Whatever else is yet deficient in my debt, my gallery of pictures will fully cover." *

* Gotzkowsky paid his debt to Russia with 30,000 dollars, a set of valuable brilliants, and the finest pictures

"It is too much—too much!" cried Féodor; and, as if hunted by Furies, with clenched hands and threatening words, as if wishing to crush to the earth any one who would dare to detain him, he rushed out of the house.

in his gallery, which were accepted by Russia, to the value of 80,000 dollars, and laid the first and best foundation of the Imperial Picture Gallery in Petersburg. Among them were some of the best works of Titian, the most choice productions of Rubens, and one of the finest portraits Rembrandt ever painted—that of his old mother.

## TARDY GRATITUDE.

Johann Gotzkowsky, the wealthy Berlin merchant, was no longer to strive and struggle with Fate,—no longer to be a daily martyr to his endangered honour—his threatened ruin.

Like the brave Leckingen, he said to himself, "Better an end with terror, than terror without end." He preferred plunging at once into the abyss, to being cast down from point to point of the rocks.

He had notified his fall in the Gazette, and his resolution to abandon all his property to his creditors. He was to-day expecting the official assignees, to whom he was to give over ll his worldly possessions, and then he intended, along with his daughter, to leave the house which was no longer his.

Not secretly, not under shade of night, did he intend to depart; but openly, in the bright light of day, he was for the last time to cross the threshold of his once happy home, —to pass along, ruined and desolate, the streets of a city which owed so much to him, and had once called him its preserver and benefactor.

It was his doom; fall he must—but his fall should also be his revenge. For the last time he had thrown open the state apartments of his house—for the last time it was his intention to receive guests in them; but these guests were the official persons who were to inherit from him, though he was still alive, and to efface his name, before death had proclaimed it on a tombstone.

The news of his ruin had quickly circulated through Berlin, and appeared at last to have broken through the crust which had formed around so many hearts, and hardened them to the misfortunes of their benefactor. The voice of conscience for a moment overpowered that of egotism. The magistrates were ashamed of their base ingratitude; and even the pitiful Jews Ephraim and Itzig perceived that it would be wiser to avoid an éclat, and more conducive to their interest to endeavour to save Gotzkowsky from utter ruin, than to crush him quite into the dust

Instead, therefore, of the assignees of bankruptcy, whom Gotzkowsky had expected, two of the magistrates appeared, accompanied by Ephraim and Itzig, and requested to see Gotzkowsky.

He received them in his state aparments, with his children by his side. He advanced to greet them, not like a man humbled and oppressed by misfortune, but with a noble and lofty aspect. As a ruler receives his vassals, thus did Gotzkowsky receive the magistrates, and, on meeting his scornful and searching glance, they cast down their eyes in shame and confusion.

"We are come as a deputation from the magistrates," said one of them.

"I have nothing more to do with those gentlemen," said Gotzkowsky, scornfully.

"Gotzkowsky, do not persevere in your anger," said the Stadt Rath, in an almost g tone; "the magistrates, in acknowledgment of your former distinguished services to the city, are prepared willingly to pay the sum you demand."

Gotzkowsky proudly shook his head. "But I am no longer prepared to receive it," said he; "the time is gone by; you cannot now buy your freedom from my claim—you must ever remain my debtors."

"You will hear us, at least," said Itzig; "we come as ambassadors from the Jewish community."

"We are empowered to help you," added Ephraim. "We intend to give you whatever money or credit you may require, simply for the regular interest and your acknowledgment, that your house may thus be saved from falling."

Gotzkowsky's large, intelligent eyes rested for a moment with a thoughtful expression on Ephraim's face, and the slight, satirical smile which was visible on the Jew's lips seemed to strengthen Gotzkowsky's resolution, and to give him fresh courage.

"My house has failed!" said he coolly; and,

on seeing the horror imprinted on their faces, he repeated, almost as if rejoicing to say it again, "Yes! my house is bankrupt! The document is already sent off in which I announce to the magistrates and to the merchants the stoppage of my firm, and declare myself bankrupt."

"You dare not do this—you shall not!" cried Itzig, furiously.

"It is not possible that you should venture to inflict such a disgrace on the city!" exclaimed the Stadt Rath, with a dignified air. "We cannot suffer posterity to say of us that the city of Berlin permitted one of her noblest citizens to sink into misery and ruin."

"It will be well for me when that is said," cried Gotzkowsky; "for my name and my honour will thus be rescued."

"The magistrates rejoice in proving their gratitude," said the other.

"The Jewish community also are so glad!" squeaked forth Itzig. "They are both ready and willing to help you."

Gotzkowsky looked at him with the most undisguised contempt.

"Which means," said he, "that you have discovered it will be much to your own advantage that I should not fail. You hold heavy bills payable by me, and, if I fail, you will only receive a small part of the debt; while, if I am carried through the present crisis, the bills will be paid in full. You affect to be magnanimous, whereas you are only selfish; I refuse to accept your offers. You turned a deaf ear to my entreaties formerly—you shall lose your money; let this be your punishment and my revenge—you have stabbed me to the heart, and in return I attack you on the only spot where you are vulnerable. I strike at your avarice; you came too late; I am now a bankrupt—my bills no longer circulate or are available; but my honour does not expire with my firm."

All were silent, and looked at each other with knit brows.

Only one looked up at Gotzkowsky with a clear bright eye; it was Ephraim, who, remembering his conversation with Gotzkowsky, said triumphantly to himself, "He has evidently followed my advice—he has taken care of his own interests."

Itzig was the most furious of all. "Are you resolved to ruin us?" said he, in a rage. "Are you determined to be ungrateful? The Jews very little deserved that from you, after the splendid brilliant they so nobly presented to you—what will the world say to that?"

"The world will know why I am ruined, and will condemn *you*, not me," said Gotzkowky. "Leave me; but first take possession of all I have, for nothing here is any longer mine; I despise riches and luxuries—I shall now be poor; but peace dwells with poverty. I turn my back for ever on this mansion and all its splendours, and, when I cross its threshold, I take nothing with me save this silver laurel wreath, the golden Leipzig goblet, and my two beloved children."

He stretched out his hands to Elise and Bertram with a bright smile.

"Come, my children, let us go hence to

commence our pilgrimage in all the happiness of obscurity. Let us shake the dust from our feet and be free and unencumbered, for we are poor, yet rich in love; we are no longer dependent on the prejudices, passions, and criticisms of others; we have no cause to be ashamed of our poverty, for we are blameless—it is for others to cast down their eyes before us, for our privations loudly speak against their probity; but, when death comes to call me, then deck my cold forehead with this wreath of silver oak leaves, which the city of Berlin presented to me, and write on my coffin "Such is the gratitude of the world!"

Raised to his full height, leaning on his children, Gotzkowsky for the last time traversed his splendid saloons, with all their luxuries and fine paintings and statues; no one dared to detain him. Shame and remorse, rage and fear, had stunned them.

"Let us go! let us go!" said Gotzkowsky, impatiently, to Elise and Bertram, "I have a horror of this house and its glitter."

"Yes, father, we will go hence," whispered

Elise, throwing her arm round her father's neck.

Thus they passed into the street.

How refreshing the pure air seemed to his weary frame; how mild, and yet how cheeringly, the blue sky looked down on him!

Gotzkowsky gazed up at it; he no longer saw the crowds assembled before his door, or perhaps he chose not to see them, thinking they were only part of the idle curious mob whom misfortune always attracts, and who find an interest and occupation in the spectacle of grief and lamentation.

But this time Gotzkowsky was in error; they were indeed only poor people standing in the street at his door, but their faces were sympathising, and their glances sorrowful. They had heard of Gotzkowsky's troubles, and had hastened to his door, not from curiosity but from sympathy; they were the poor workmen of his manufactories, to whom Gotzkowsky had been a benefactor, and friend, and adviser. It was those industrious but lowly poor whom he had supported and comforted, who now stood before him, to wish Gotzkowsky, their generous friend and noble master, a last kind farewell. They could, indeed, bring him no aid, for they had neither gold nor treasures, but they brought him their love and their tears.

At the head of this troop of workmen stood Balthasar with his young wife, and, though his eyes were dimmed by tears, he quickly recognised the master to whom he owed so much, and, though grief weighed heavily on his faithful heart, yet he commanded himself, and called out, "Long live Gotzkowsky, our friend and father!"

"Hurrah! long live Gotzkowsky!" shouted the crowd, not joyfully, but in tones of sadness, and half choked with tears.

Gotzkowsky's face beamed with joy, and he stretched out his hand to Balthasar with a grateful smile.

"I thank you, my dear friends—I thank you from my heart!" said he, deeply moved, "you have often cheered at the sound of my name, but never with such balm to my heart as this day."

"Never was it more heartfelt or more sincere," said Balthasar, pressing Gotzkowsky's hand to his lips; "you have been more than a parent to all of us, and we often almost regretted your being so rich and powerful, as it prevented our being able to show you how truly we loved you. Now, when you are no longer so, we can prove our attachment by at least working for you. We have already agreed what to do. Each of us is to give one day's labour, and its wages are to go to you, and, as we are two hundred and seventy workmen, this will at least prevent your being utterly destitute, father Gotzkowsky!"

Gotzkowsky looked at them with heartfelt gratitude. "I thank you, my kind friends," said he, deeply moved, "and, though I cannot accept your noble offer, yet do not believe that I am ungrateful, or that the beauty and kindness of such a sacrifice are lost on me. Who can say that I am poor when I am rich in love such as yours, my children?"

The carriage now drew up to the door, which Bertram had brought to take them to their new and humble abode.

"You are determined to leave us for ever?" said Balthasar, sadly.

"No, my children, I mean to remain with you, to live in the midst of you," said Gotzkowsky, "only I must exchange this large house for a quiet cottage."

"Come, friends," cried Balthasar, "let us at least escort father Gotzkowsky to his new home. The city of Berlin shall see that it is only the rich who are ungrateful, and that the poor never forget their benefactors and friends. Take out the horses, we will drag Gotzkowsky through the streets."

A thundering hurrah from the crowd was the answer, and in an instant they set to work. The horses were unharnessed, and twelve of the most powerful workmen joyfully made ready for the labour of love.

In vain Gotzkowsky entreated them to desist, and not to make him an object of universal curiosity. The people would not listen to him; they were resolved to give a public proof of their esteem to their benefactor. They carried him into the carriage almost by force, and insisted on Elise and Bertram placing themselves by his side.

At last the procession moved forwards, the crowd shouting as they went along. Wherever the carriage passed, by lowly houses or poor cottages, the small, dusty windows were thrown open, and weather beaten faces looked out, and hard, horny hands waved their caps.

The forsaken, cruelly treated, ruined Gotzkowsky, enjoyed still a noble triumph on this day. The people brought him their joyful homage, and his heart was comforted in its sorrow.

## THE AUCTION.

All was ended and over — the curtain had fallen—Gotzkowsky had closed his brilliant career, and retired into obscurity and forgetfulness.

His ruin formed a topic of conversation for several days among the worthy inhabitants of Berlin, but it had been long superseded by some other novelty, and people passed by his deserted house and its closed windows, without either sympathy or malice. Gotzkowsky's once splendid dwelling had been purchased by the King to form a porcelain manufactory, the same which Gotzkowsky had founded, and which was now to be carried on at the royal expense.

Months passed away. How much had been changed in this short space of time! How many tears had been shed during its course! how many hopes had been crushed!

Elise was now Bertram's wife, and lived with him and her father in the small neat cottage which they had selected, in a distant suburb of the city.

The three had taken possession of the small, low-roofed rooms which were now to form their home, with the firm resolution not to allow themselves to be disturbed by the petty privations and annoyances which must inevitably fall to their share. They submitted to them with cheerfulness and equanimity, proudly disregarding the loss of former luxuries, and consoling themselves by the thought that no one could rob them of the sacred and precious capital of their mutual love.

Their honour, too, and their good name, remained untouched, for every one knew Gotzkowsky's hard fate; that he had not fallen from any fault of his own, but through the force of unfortunate circumstances, and the malice of others. He had good cause to complain of men, but they could not do so of him; his creditors had been eventually satisfied, he had given up all he had in the world, and every one had been paid in full.

He could pass along the streets with as proud a step and as lofty an air as before; no one could follow him with taunts and reproaches. He had no cause to blush for his poverty, for this very poverty was a proof of his undeserved misfortunes, and his own honourable conduct.

He repeated this constantly to himself, and yet it pained him to go through the streets so solitary, and tears involuntarily rushed to his eyes one day when, in passing his former residence, he saw the gates open, and carriages standing there as formerly, and the same rich and distinguished people, with their cold, unsympathising aristocratic faces, who had in other days crowded his saloons, and bowed down before him.

Those who had formerly come to Gotzkowsky's splendid banquets, had now come to a sale by auction in his house.

The velvet chairs and couches, the soft carpets and gold embroidered curtains, the chandeliers of rock crystal and bronze, the pictures and statues, the gold and silver plate, and the rare and precious services of porcelain, were all to be put up to auction for what they would fetch.

There is something very melancholy and touching in a sale by auction; it always proclaims either the death or the ruin and entire breaking up of a family; either the loss of some loved one or of domestic happiness; the melancholy fragments of a shattered existence, or the sad remains of a once brilliant life. When the day of sale arrives, sacred privacy and the harmony of family life is over, the hearth is no longer the hearth of peace and cheerfulness—all is now coldness and desolation.

The doors are thrown open, and the curious crowd stream into the house, spying into every corner and every room with cold searching eyes, trying the sofa and armchair on which perhaps yesterday a poor widow had sunk down while weeping bitter tears for the loss of an idolised husband, and a lost home; they look around the boudoir and the other apartments, once the scenes of love and happiness, with an unmoved heart, and soon all the various articles of furniture are scattered far and wide, one to a castle, another to a cottage, some to the pawnbroker's shop, while others go to adorn the new saloons of some wealthy Jew.

All the splendours of Gotzkowsky's early days were to be put up to auction to-day. On this account, therefore, were there so many carriages before his door, and so many rich people again visiting his house, crowding his saloons, along with brokers and speculators, all striving to obtain some portion of these valuables with the least possible expenditure.

No one heeded the figure leaning against the doorway, who, with his hat pressed low on his brows, and his cloak dragged up so as to cover his face, stood there bowed down with sorrow and bitter regret. No one saw how he shrank when the auctioneer roughly handled the various beautiful works of art, and stimulated the public to purchase them. It was indeed torture to him to visit this funeral feast of his past existence; and yet he could not tear himself away. He felt as if transfixed there by some demoniacal power, to witness this desecration of the home which he had so fondly loved, and of which he had once been so proud. In the weariness of his inactive and dreary life it was a kind of excitement, rousing him from his gloomy regrets, to be an eyewitness of the desolation of his house and the distribution of his property; and yet every stroke of the hammer of the auctioneer, fell like a blow on his own heart, and made it bleed.

Occasionally, when well known voices struck his ear, he would raise his head a little and look at the bidders, but their cold, careless faces made him shrink. How many there were whom he had once called his friends, or whom he had benefited! Now they crowded like birds of prey to tear asunder the remains of his past life; they were eagerly purchasing his most cherished treasures; and, forgetful of his sufferings, gloated on the objects put up for sale, their whole thoughts engrossed by the wish to purchase them as cheaply as possible, and to be able to boast that they possessed some memorial of the once wealthy and distinguished Gotzkowsky.

When Gotzkowsky witnesssed their unfeeling demeanour, he felt ashamed that he had ever smiled so kindly on these false friends, ever trusted in their friendship, and believed their assurances of attachment.

He rose to go, for he felt that the bitter lesson, though painful, had been beneficial to him; that his fond regrets had passed away, and that he was now strengthened to endure his fate.

Never had he gone with a firmer step through the streets, than when he returned from the auction in his palace to his small obscure cottage; never had he more sincerely pitied mankind, or detested their hypocrisy and want of kindness, than on this day.

And yet it pained him to cross the threshold of his quiet, silent dwelling, and again to find his powers of body and mind circumscribed within its obscure walls, and to be constrained to resume a vegetating life of idleness and *ennui.*

It was a source of never ending sorrow, in all the strength and energy of his matured powers to be condemned to entire repose, and to be doomed to have no other occupation than to drag on his weary existence, to eat, to sleep, and to dream of the past. He felt he had the power, mentally and bodily, to create, and to labour, and to combine, and yet he must remain idle and inactive, supported by the energies of others, though they were his own children.

But they worked for him with such joy and such love!

Bertram had accepted a situation as book-keeper in a commercial house, and his salary sufficed to support them all. Much economy was necessary, much care indispensable, to cover their necessary expenses; but Elise was both active and energetic. A spoiled child of luxury, surrounded by servants, she had learned nothing of the smaller realities of life, none of the cares and anxieties of a household; but the instinct of woman had quickly taught her this knowledge, and she soon mastered all its details and difficulties.

It was charming to see this lovely young creature so delicately reared, once so assiduously waited on and so luxuriously attired, now as cheerful and calm as ever, fulfilling the duties of her family, and replacing, by neatness and good management, what was deficient in elegance and beauty.

Elise was indeed a changed creature, and never since the day she became Bertram's wife had a cloud crossed her sweet face, or a single tear dimmed her bright eyes. She invariably looked bright and cheerful, she had always a cordial smile to welcome home her husband and her father, and ever words of love and hope to cheer them. Never did she utter one word of complaint or of regret at the many privations to which she was obliged to submit, nor at the great wealth which she had lost for ever.

Elise felt herself rich, for she truly loved her husband, not with the ardent and absorbing passion she had once felt for Féodor, and which had caused her so many fond delusions and so many bitter tears, but with the gentle, beneficent affection which never dies away, because esteem, and gratitude, and the perception of moral excellence always impart to it fresh impulse, and fresh nourishment.

Bertram was not only her brother, but her lover and friend—her comforter and her counsellor; she was always certain of meeting with sympathy, aid, and consolation, as well as encouragement, from him; she could securely build on his noble heart, as on a rock,—a heart so strong in the struggle of life, and yet so soft in love for her, which had never doubted her and never would forsake her.

She had given him her whole and undivided love, and she earnestly strove to reward his noble conduct towards her father by the untiring and loving devotion of her whole life—too little, she thought, to testify her gratitude to him for having sacrificed his whole property to rescue the name and honour of her father from shame and disgrace. She no longer wished for pomp and pleasures—this humble cottage, illumined by the light of her husband's love, and calm and peaceful happiness, seemed to her a temple of peace and holy rest,—encircled by Bertram's arms, her wishes never strayed beyond their humble roof.

But Gotzkowsky could not bring himself into this state of resignation; each day that passed away in idleness and inactivity increased his impatience; sometimes he could have cried out aloud in his despair, and in the fulness of his grief.

He had during his whole life devoted himself to the interests of his fellow creatures and toiled for them; how had he deserved thus to fall from his high estate, while others, who had become rich by knavery and cunning, by scheming, and unscrupulously taking advantage of their neighbours, were seen driving through the streets in the pomp of brilliant equipages, surrounded by all the attractions of wealth and splendour? He saw them pass by, while slowly going on his way, with a heavy heart and a bent figure.

He had sunk, but Ephraim had risen all the more. Gotzkowsky had become poor because he was honest—Ephraim had become rich because he was a usurer—his firm was ruined, and Ephraim's bills circulated far and wide. What did the Jew care that his name was branded by the people, or for their indignation at the leaden money to which Ephraim had so cleverly contrived to give the appearance of silver, or that they loathed his very name?

At length Gotzkowsky roused himself to action, and hardened his heart to an act of revenge—he was determined to have his revenge on the men who had first ruined and then forsaken him; he was resolved at least to remind those who now passed him without recognition in all their pomp and pride, of their baseness and ingratitude.

He would accuse no one, but his whole life was an accusation not only against individuals, but against communities, against cities, nay, even against the King himself.

They had all been equally thankless to him; they were all still his debtors; before the world he would hurl in their faces their meanness, malice, and dishonesty, and humble them in their pride by recalling the past.

For this purpose he wrote the history of his

life; but not with scorn and malice. He did not dip his pen in gall, he made no abusive remarks, no contumelious reproaches; what he did was, calmly, simply, and truthfully to depict his life and his actions, always, where it was necessary, substantiating the accuracy of his statements by references to various documents and acts which he quoted.

The concluding paragraph runs thus:

"I have always acted like a true Christian and a good patriot—I would act precisely in the same way if I were to live my life over again; only I would be more cautious in ascertaining the real character of those whom I benefited, and in whose worth I placed entire confidence. Peace of mind, and the proud feeling of a good conscience, which innocence and the sense of honour ever bestow, are too precious for me ever to choose the path of vice and success, in preference to that of integrity and misfortune."* But the very simplicity, truth, and moderation of this "Biography of a Patriotic Merchant" caused it to make an im-

* With these words Gotzkowsky closes his biography.

mense sensation, and again the long-forgotten and ill-used Gotzkowsky became the universal subject of conversation, not only in Berlin, but through the whole of Germany.

Every one read the book—every one wished to have the malicious satisfaction of seeing how distinguished people—such as magistrates, nobles, and princes—could have placed themselves under the deepest obligations to this man, and yet have allowed him to be ruined without an effort to save him.

The natural consequence was that this book, although written in such a reserved and modest spirit, caused much anger.

Gotzkowsky accused no one—but facts were accusations enough. His present need and poverty condemned the proud citizens, and showed the world their baseness and cold-heartedness. The King also was included in the circle of ingrates. The King! for whom Gotzkowsky had purchased pictures to the amount of a hundred thousand ducats, and of this sum he had only been repaid one hundred and fifty thousand dollars. If his book had contained the slightest untruth, or even any perverted facts, he would have been attacked as a calumniator, and as having traduced and offended royalty itself.*

But Gotzkowsky had told simple facts; he could not therefore be accused of falsehood or malice. The only resource therefore was to prohibit the publication of his History. All the different booksellers in Berlin were obliged to deliver up their copies, and Gotzkowsky himself received the order to send back his own.†

* The Prussian money, so long as Ephraim farmed the mint, became every day worse, and at last consisted only of lead; so the people called this class of dollar either a "lead trap" or an "Ephraimite."

† Gotzkowsky begins with the following words:—"I know that there will be various opinions as to my actions. I shall appear very absurd in the eyes of many, because I used my prosperity for the benefit of others, and not for my own. They will say a man who knew the world, and a merchant moreover, whose chief merit and aim should be to become rich and to found a great family, gave so little heed to selfishness, and devoted himself so entirely to visionary schemes of magnanimity and love towards

He did so. He gave up the book; but they could not deprive him of his memory. *He* could not give up his recollections of the past to those who persecuted him, because they were forced to blush when they saw him.

His memory remained clear and faithful, and was his resource and consolation; but he was now very much reduced in circumstances, and gaunt poverty, with all its miseries, humiliations, and privations, drew near.

Gotzkowsky's book had again revived the wrath of those who had envied and hated him

his fellow-creatures, that we can scarcely forgive him for calling himself a philosopher. Others will condemn my actions as weak, inconsiderate, or arising from vanity; but, so long as I have the consciousness that I have acted like a true Christian and an upright patriot, I can afford to despise all these harsh judgments. I would act in precisely the same manner if I were to live my whole life over again! The repose of spirit, the cheerfulness, which innocence and the consciousness of good conduct impart, are too highly prized by me ever to make me for a moment regret, that instead of selfish motives I have ever been guided by a disinterested love towards my fellow-creatures."

in the days of his prosperity; and they had their revenge. Not on him, for he had nothing more which they could seize—no wealth, no influence, no credit, nor even, in their mercantile eyes, honour; but they revenged themselves on his family—on his son-in-law.

The rich manufacturer whose bookkeeper Bertram was, deprived him of his situation, and, in accordance with an agreement among the other merchants, Bertram could not procure any other office.

How was he now to support his family? How gladly he would have worked as a common workman to support his wife, her father, and his child, who looked at him with such loving blue eyes, little heeding in its infantine innocence the sorrows which preyed on its parents. But nowhere would they employ Bertram—every place was closed to the son-in-law of Gotzkowsky, whose book had brought to shame the merchants, the magistrates of Berlin, and even the King himself.

Thus condemned to inactivity, they asked each other with a shudder what was to become of them, and how this life of misery and want was to end.

While Bertram and Elise were thus dejected and despairing, Gotzkowsky's face suddenly brightened. Long had he walked up and down in thoughtful silence; but now his eye beamed with intelligence as in former days, and proud energy breathed in his every gesture. Elise saw him with surprise take out of a drawer the last memorials which remained of happier days—they were the silver wreath, richly mounted in brilliants, which the city of Berlin had given him, and the gold goblet which the city of Leipzig had presented to him, in token of their everlasting gratitude.

Gotzkowsky gazed at them long with earnest attention. He went out, and Elise was alone, to weep and to pray to God for aid and for strength to bear her misfortunes, and to console Bertram when he returned home after his usual fruitless search for a situation.

Some hours later Gotzkowsky came back, his face still bright, and bearing the impress of the decision and energy of former days.

He pressed his children to his heart.

"Can we really think ourselves very poor when we are still together, true and loving as ever?" said he. "I say that we are still rich, for our hearts are warm and our honour has never yet been tainted; but we have so far been in error that we have endeavoured to conceal our real poverty by an outward appearance of respectability; we have striven to be poor and yet to be happy, in a city where we were once so differently situated—a city which has been our ruin. Poverty is bitter, indeed, within the walls of a town, but not so in the region of nature; in the solitude of rural life peace and rest are to be found. Come, my children, let us leave this hard and ungrateful town for ever—let us have strength of mind to become children of nature; leaving for ever all the glitter and frivolity of a town life, let us wander away, not over the seas, not into a desert, but to a cottage in a forest. I have got rid of the last remains of grandeur, and the silver crown and the golden goblet have been of some use at last, for they have given us the means of commencing a new existence. Bertram, have you courage to start afresh in life, and to become a peasant along with me?"

Bertram smiled. "I have both courage and inclination," said he cheerfully, "for I have health, and strength, and good will to work."

"And you, Elise, are you too proud to bring up your child in the rank of a peasant's son?"

Elise kissed her child fondly, and placed it in her father's arms; "Let us make him a good and honest man," said she, "a man who will one day equal yourself and his father, he will then conquer both the world and its trials and be happy."

"Oh, I knew well that I might rely on you both," said Gotzkowsky, "and now I know what we must do; we are rich enough to purchase a piece of land in some remote corner of the world, which we will cultivate ourselves, and build a cottage on it. The produce of my valuables is sufficient for this purpose, and what the sale of our present furniture will fetch will more than defray the expenses of our journey; prepare yourselves, my children—to-morrow we leave this for the wilds of Silesia. In the mountains there we will seek out some still, secluded valley at their base, where the peasant strangers can build a hut. There we will forget the past, and cast away for ever all its pains and sorrows, as if it were a mere legend of our youth. Come, my children, let us seek our home with God and with nature, and be contented and happy. Do you remember, Elise, my relating to you once the story of my childhood, how as a boy I lay hungry and thirsty on the high way, and a hand appeared to me out of a cloud of dust and threw me an alms which saved me from perishing of hunger? I have again lain on the highway, wretched and starving, but the hand now extended to me did not come out of a cloud, but from the bright sky, and it has given me, not alms, but love—the love of my children; it has restored me to hope and strength, and I can look up in humble faith to God, as becomes a Christian. In the days of my pride I trusted to my own strength, which must always prove a broken reed; misfortune has taught me where true strength alone lies, and I humbly venture to hope that my remorse, when I think of my impatience and despair under chastisement, has purified and sanctified my being, and that my heartfelt repentance and prayers for acceptance, in deep humility through our blessed Redeemer, have not been in vain. I can reverence our heavenly Father and look up to Him in his works. God dwells and speaks to us in his creation. Let us go to the sublime hills and forests, and seek God there as our Father and our Friend, and serve Him earnestly and love Him with our whole hearts, now and till the hour of our death."

* * * * *

They set forth, and did as Gotzkowsky had said. They went to Silesia, and bought a piece of land in the mountain district, and worked in linen blouses like honest peasants, and built a pretty cottage, and lived there in peace and happiness and harmony.

The world forgot them—Gotzkowsky's name was never heard; but history has preserved his memory as an example of the most noble and disinterested patriotism, and also as a melancholy instance of the ingratitude of men.

Gotzkowsky's book, too, still remains and bears witness for him, and in reading it deep emotion and sadness must fill every heart, and his own epitaph must recur to every mind, "Such is the gratitude of the world!"

THE END.

CPSIA information can be obtained
at www.ICGtesting.com
Printed in the USA
LVHW042017130323
741532LV00003B/464

9 783375 151706